IN A
DRY LAND

SOPHIA & SONIA SAMANTAROY

ST MARY & MOSES ABBEY PRESS

In a Dry Land

Designed & Published by:
St. Mary & St. Moses Abbey Press
101 S Vista Dr, Sandia, TX 78383
stmabbeypress.com

Cover image design by Sheren Iskander (concept initially inspired by Sara Ibrahim).

Library of Congress Cataloging-in-Publication Data

Names: Samantaroy, Sonia, author. | Samantaroy, Sophia, author.
Title: In a dry land / by Sonia and Sophia Samantaroy.
Description: Sandia, TX : St. Mary & St. Moses Abbey Press, [2022]
Identifiers: LCCN 2022010378 (print) | LCCN 2022010379 (ebook) | ISBN
    9781939972446 (paperback) | ISBN 9781939972453 (epub)
Subjects: CYAC: Christian life--Fiction. | Survival--Fiction. | Mojave
    Desert--Fiction. | LCGFT: Christian fiction.
Classification: LCC PZ7.1.S25445 In 2022 (print) | LCC PZ7.1.S25445
    (ebook) | DDC [Fic]--dc23
LC record available at https://lccn.loc.gov/2022010378
LC ebook record available at https://lccn.loc.gov/2022010379

To all the wild, whimsical, and wonderful Coptic kids out there—you are the future.

Chapter One

They wandered in the wilderness in a desolate way. (Psalm 107:4)

"We're about half an hour away from the monastery," Andrew, the kids' tall and lanky Sunday School teacher, said over his shoulder. "Do you guys want to read the Sixth Hour of the *Agpeya*? It's almost exactly noon."

Finn and his friends rolled their eyes.

"I think I'll stick to my spiritual book," Theodore said, covering his comic book with a saint book he had in his backpack. He gave his friends a sly look and ducked under the two books.

Toni snickered and passed Finn the blue part of Theodore's Switch console. Finn felt guilty for playing video games instead of praying the Sixth-Hour Psalms but ignored it. He reasoned that he would be spending three long weeks at the Monastery of Saint Moses—without Nintendo Switches. Video games would be a distraction for the kids, so as soon as they arrived, Theodore's precious Switches would be whisked away by the Sunday School teachers. Andrew looked into the rearview mirror, shook his head, and continued driving the bus along the bumpy unpaved road.

The entire junior high, fifth through eighth grade,

was going on this trip. The eighth graders were especially known for their pranks. On the last retreat, they had put potato chips in everyone's shoes. And it was just his luck that out of all the kids, Toni, Theodore, and himself were chosen to be stuck on the bus with the extra luggage and the air conditioning that was on way too high. All the other kids were ahead in other buses, probably having fun playing games while Finn was freezing.

"Hey Andrew! Can you turn down the AC?" asked Finn with chattering teeth.

Andrew looked apologetic. "Sorry man, it only has one setting."

Finn, Toni, and Theodore were making their way through the Mojave Desert from their homes in Virginia with their Sunday School. This was their first summer trip with their church. Finn was glad they had at least flown most of the way there. At twelve years old, he had never been on a plane ride without his parents, but the six and half hours were filled with watching movies, reading books, and playing games with his two best friends. But the bus ride was getting tiresome.

"I don't even want to go to a monastery, it's the start of summer!" Finn whispered, not looking up from the video game.

"Yeah same," Toni said. "I'm missing softball training for this. The high school girls were going to come and help with conditioning, but then my mom was like 'you're going to a monastery in California. It'll be fun.'" Toni rolled her eyes. "I was thinking that while I'm here my *Tayta* can visit me. Even though she is only two hours away from the monastery, there's no main highway—just dirt roads—so it's too remote for her to visit."

"That's cool that your grandma lives in a desert, but you're not the only one missing something," Theodore grumbled, looking up from his comic. "My cousins had invited me to go to the Red Sea in Egypt with them. Now I can't go."

"I don't understand why our parents think that a visit to a monastery across the country is a fun thing to do over the summer," Finn said, moving his fingers faster on the control. "I'm about to be in first place, Antonia!"

"Don't call me that, *Phineas*," Toni said, giving Finn a look.

Finn laughed as Toni's character shot ahead of him.

It was all his Mama's fault that he was on this bus, but he was glad that his two best friends were coming along. The three of them had been friends since first grade.

He took a break from Mario Kart to look out the window into the desert. Stubby shrubs stubbornly resisted the wind blowing across the arid landscape. In the distance rose imposing cliffs littered with more small shrubs. He was glad now for the frigid air conditioning—the alternative would cook him in minutes.

"Guys look, there's a Joshua Tree!" Finn said. After reading about these cacti in the botany book he got from the school book fair, he was surprised to actually see the rare plant. "Joshua trees can live longer than humans can—I bet that one right there is older than your Tayta. Now they're super rare. I think my book said that Joshua Trees are losing their habitat because of climate change," he said, shaking his head. He wished people could understand that plants were just as valuable as cute pandas or dignified elephants.

"I didn't know a plant could lose its habitat," said Theodore with a frown. Before Finn could go into further detail, Andrew cut in.

"Google Maps is telling me to take a shortcut," said Andrew over his shoulder. "We'll get there ten minutes early."

Finn and his friends grinned at each other. They just wanted to get out of the bus. It had dull blue seats and was half the size of the yellow bus they rode to school every day, but the assorted duffel bags, suitcases, and backpacks in the rear took up a third of the seating space. Theodore put his Switch back in his bag and Toni started collecting the half-eaten snacks they had left around their seats. Relieved that he would be out of the bus soon, Finn also started to pack up.

Andrew maneuvered the white bus to the right, off the well-worn dirt road in favor of a barely visible trail.

How could Google Maps have a shortcut? Finn thought. *There aren't any roads!*

All Finn could see were more shrubs, a few cacti, and a Joshua Tree here and there—the landscape soon lost its initial appeal as the minutes ticked by. He also began to see large red boulders near the base of a cliff. Taking in the scenery, Finn noticed that the dirt road they were on was steeply descending through a small canyon. The path they were on now looked almost like a dry riverbed. He strained out of his seat to see the road they were just on, but it had disappeared over the canyon wall. Finn couldn't help but wonder if they should have stuck with the other buses.

This was a view he was not expecting when he heard they were going to California. Finn was expecting beaches, palm trees, and surfers, not a monastery in the middle of the Mojave Desert, a place known to get up to 120 degrees in the summer. Finn missed Virginia, with its sometimes-snowy winters and beautiful autumns. Now he was in the Mojave Desert, just next to Death Valley, *Death* Valley. The place known for its extreme weather. Everything here looked like it wanted to curl up and die.

Finn heard Andrew mutter something about it being 40 minutes and still no sign of the monastery.

CLUNK! CLUNK! BOOM!

The bus suddenly lurched and then sputtered to a stop. The kids looked up. Andrew frowned and got out of the bus to check under the hood.

"Well this is great," Finn said, looking out to see Andrew peering into the smoking engine.

"Imagine getting stranded in the Mojave Desert," Theodore said, and the three of them chuckled nervously.

"I bet I can help with this," said Toni standing up. She had once helped her dad replace a tire on the way back from softball practice. She was proud that she could change a tire—she didn't know anyone her age who could.

"That's not the same. I bet Andrew can take care of this one. Didn't he help jumpstart that car in the church parking lot once?" said Theodore.

The kids nervously looked out at Andrew, who was sweating in the desert heat. His skinny figure was bent over the hood as he ran his fingers through his damp hair. Andrew paced around the hood, occasionally looking back up towards the kids with a worried glance. When he caught the kids staring back, he grinned and gave them a thumbs up. They were starting to sweat too—the bus quickly heated up without the blasting AC.

Andrew stopped examining the engine and climbed back into the bus. He muttered to himself as he rifled through the dusty glove compartment.

"Andrew what are you looking for?" asked Toni, getting up from her seat.

"A manual or something..." said Andrew, looking distracted as he flipped through the different colored papers for a couple more seconds. "Nothing," he muttered and slammed the compartment shut. "Well, I don't know if it would have helped anyways," said Andrew with a frustrated sigh. He tromped out the bus and started fiddling with the hood again.

Ten minutes later, Andrew came back wiping his hands on his shorts, leaving black grease marks. "Sorry gang, the engine is completely dead. I'm going to try to call the other teachers." He took out his iPhone and then shoved it back into his pocket with a groan. "There's no service. You know what, I think I'm just going to head to the monastery and get some help," he said, getting flustered. Andrew was new to teaching Sunday School and had never led a youth expedition.

"Wait you're just going to leave us by ourselves!" protested Theodore.

"The other buses should already be there by now. Just

stay put and I'll be back in no later than 30 minutes, I think it's half a mile away. Read the Agpeya—you were supposed to do that earlier."

The kids nodded mutely as Andrew got out of the bus.

"Wait, Andrew!" yelled Theodore. "Take an extra water bottle!" handing him a plastic bottle from his backpack.

Andrew smiled, "Thanks man. Stay in the bus and don't go anywhere. I'll be back by the time you finish the Sixth Hour," he said with a wink.

He stepped out of the van and into the vastness of the American Southwest. They watched his figure grow small and then disappear into the seemingly safe desert.

In his wake was silence.

Chapter Two

Finn bit at his fingernails. A sense of dread grew in the pit of his stomach. Andrew had gone to get help almost two hours ago, and they were all restless. Theodore's Switch was dead, and the bus was unbearably hot now that there was no air conditioning. Finn wished for the freezing bus they had not too long ago. *Why did Andrew just leave them?* He pushed back his sweaty hair in irritation. Finn stared enviously at Toni's sports headband that kept the sweat out of her eyes.

Toni had opened all the windows and the door, but they still stayed in the hot bus—that was Andrew's parting command.

"Guys, why hasn't Andrew come back yet?" asked Finn, finally voicing his concern. "It's getting dark," he said, looking out into the desert.

"I'm sure he's fine," said Toni, finding another bag of Doritos and offering one to Theodore. "Maybe he's hanging out with the monks and eating *ful mudammas*," she said laughing. She hated that mushy bean dish.

Theodore declined the chips and started to look out the window too. "I agree with Finn, he should be back by now. Plus, we're in the desert, there could be dangerous animals and it's going to get cold during the night. By now, he could have been eaten by a savage mountain lion!"

"I read that mountain lions are one of the only animals

that actively hunt humans," Finn said, pushing his damp brown hair out of his eyes again. Finn had made sure to read up on the wildlife of the Southwest. He had thought that one of the cool things about the Monastery was the surrounding wildlife. Now, he wished he hadn't read about the way mountain lions attack humans on bike trails. From behind.

"I mean I've only seen a few mountain lions prowling around my Tayta's backyard in California," Toni said, grinning at Theodore and winking at Finn. "It's going to get cold soon since we're in the desert. Good thing there is an entire backseat full of suitcases packed with clothes."

"We're going to poke through other people's stuff?" asked Theodore, appalled.

"Theo, it's getting late," Toni argued. "When the sun goes down the scorching heat is replaced by the cold."

She was right. With the sun sinking behind the canyon walls, Finn could feel the heat slipping out of the bus. His legs were already covered in goosebumps. He was startled that the temperature could go from boiling to freezing in an hour. They needed the extra clothing.

"The Mojave Desert gets to be around 50 degrees at night," added Toni, spotting Finn's goosebumps. She too had researched the desert by calling her grandmother before she left. Even though she relished her knowledge about the desert, she felt like it was all bad news.

"Yeah, I guess you're right," said Theodore.

With that, Toni got to work pulling the heavy suitcases from the back and the boys scavenged through the clothes pulling out socks, hoodies, and sweatpants. They also grabbed any water or snacks they found. The kids were exhausted, but they had a hefty pile of clothes, a good amount of chip bags, and some packets of cookies. By the time they were done, it was completely dark outside. The temperature continued to drop. Toni was right. The desert wasn't a place to mess around.

After a sad dinner of Pringles and Oreos, Finn looked to Theodore, who was silent in the back. He looked like he was about to cry, just like when his cat passed away and he pretended everything was fine.

"Dude, are you okay?" asked Finn, slipping into the row.

Toni slid in on the end, making them all squished on the seats.

"I'm freaking out," Theodore whispered. "We're in the middle of the desert, it's dark, there are carnivorous, people-eating animals, we're alone, and no one is going to find us!" He continued breathing hard and put his head in his hands. "Where in the world is Andrew?!" Theodore let out a half-sob.

Hearing their situation aloud made the kids fall silent.

Theodore continued to breathe heavily. "We're going to die out here and I never said goodbye to my parents and sister and kitten!" He burst into tears.

"Oh, Theo," said Toni. She and Finn wrapped their arms around his trembling body. They too felt tears drip down their saddened faces. "Here, I found a couple of books in the luggage. Maybe we can read it aloud, and it'll help calm us down." She went to the front of the bus and retrieved *The Lion, the Witch, and the Wardrobe* by C.S. Lewis.

With the use of an old flashlight they found, they read

about the adventures of the four Pevensie children in the land of Narnia. Finn and Toni took turns reading the book aloud. Theodore hiccupped as he listened.

They forgot that they were in the middle of the desert, alone. They were with Aslan, Lucy, Edmund, Susan, and Peter. They were somber when Aslan was ridiculed and beaten and killed. And they were with him when he rose from the dead. They were filled with a sense of hope and peace even in the black, cold night as Aslan triumphed over the evil White Witch. Theodore, Finn, and Toni calmed down. Maybe they too could overcome the fear and uncertainty as Lucy had when Aslan was by her side.

They read through most of the book because they didn't want to stop reading. Reading the magical story kept the darkness, the scariness, away.

Reading of the epic battle by flashlight, the kids were immersed in the story. Out of the dark, they heard a faint whisper.

I am with you.

Each child heard it in their own head, but each was too unsure of what they heard to say anything to each other.

Toni finished reading with the Pevensies tumbling out of the wardrobe.

They decided to try and get some sleep. The kids pulled on more clothes as blankets and settled down on the bus seats, the whisper fading from their memories.

I am with you.

Again, they brushed that eerie whisper from their thoughts; they had other things to think about. Toni tried to relive her best softball game and Theodore, the time when his dad took him to his work at the hospital.

As Finn laid down on the seats, he couldn't stop thinking about their Sunday School teacher. "Do you think we should look for Andrew tomorrow?" asked Finn, trying to get comfortable on the lightly cushioned seats.

"I could go and try to find him tomorrow," offered Toni, yawning.

"Then you would need the rescuing. And what if he actually did find help and is coming back tomorrow?" said Theodore, from across the aisle.

"Fight me," said Toni.

"Stop bickering," mumbled Finn. "We should just stay put. My dad always told me to never move if I get lost," Finn said. "I just wish that we had a phone or something to call for help." As he drifted off into a restless sleep, the mysterious voice echoed *I am with you* in his head.

Finn was woken up by his rumbling stomach. He rubbed his sleepy eyes and checked the old leather watch his *Gidu* gave him on his tenth birthday. It was 2:43 am.

Rrrrh…

His stomach was growling angrily at him, demanding more food, but Finn didn't want to be selfish and have more food than his friends. He had never gone to bed hungry. He grabbed a small flashlight from his backpack and stepped out of the bus into the cold night. Finn tightened his hoodie straps.

Even in the darkness, the desert was alive with activity. He could hear scampering mice and owl hoots. Finn clenched his fists. All he needed to do was go to the bathroom. He tried not to think about the mountain lions and coyotes Toni had mentioned before. They could be roaming around him in the shadows. His heart thumped faster. Finn hurried to a tall cactus to pee.

This is weird, Finn thought, *I feel like I'm being watched. Don't think like that Finn, they're just overgrown cats and dogs,* he thought, swiftly heading back to the comfort of the bus.

Just as he was about to shut the doors behind him, something moved in the corner of his eye.

Finn whipped around.

A bright yellow eye hovered in the shadows only 100 feet behind him.

Oh no. Oh no no no.

In his adrenaline-filled state, Finn tried to think straight.

Why does that mountain lion only have one eye? Did it get into a fight? Oh no, it's coming towards me!

Only when the animal began stalking forward did his instincts to flee kick in.

"AHHHH!" Finn spun on his heel and pulled the door shut.

Toni and Theodore were fast asleep underneath their pile of clothes.

"Wake up!" he screamed, shaking Theodore and Toni.

"Wake up! Now!"

Theodore shifted around and looked up at him annoyed. "What are you doing?" he asked groggily.

"There's a HUGE mountain lion cougar-thingy just outside our bus!" yelled Finn, frantically. *Why didn't his friends understand that a bloodthirsty animal was coming after them?*

Just then the three kids heard growling. Then scratching sounds from the front of the bus.

"YIKES!" screamed Theodore, his eyes wide.

"Get to the back!" yelled Toni.

Without hesitating, they scrambled over the extra luggage to the back of the bus and huddled together on the far row.

There was another scratch and then Finn could hear breaking glass.

"That was the door," moaned Theodore, crouching lower in the seat. He didn't look good.

Finn and Theodore were both involuntarily shaking, their shoulders rubbing against each other.

Toni, who was on the edge, began rifling through the luggage.

"What are you doing?" hissed Theodore. "The mountain lion is going to hear us!" Hot tears were escaping from his huge chocolate eyes.

"It already smells us," she muttered. "I'd rather have a weapon than cower in fear." She paused. "Theodore! Give me your knife!"

Theodore yelped and fumbled around his pockets. "It must have fallen out!" he cried.

Finn was squished between them, his mind racing. *Had he just led a mountain lion to his friends?* He peered over Theodore and out of the window but couldn't see anything in the moonless night. The rustling and growling sound was getting louder and louder.

THUMP

The bus shuddered.

He froze. Finn looked over the benches and into the aisle. The glowing yellow eye stared back at him. There was a thick scar where his left eye should have been. It was a nearly seven-foot cat, with a muscular tan body and black markings decorating its ears and snout.

Theodore's jaw dropped, unable to scream. Toni carefully pulled out a hair curling wand and Finn held his breath, looking directly at the mountain lion.

The cat must have taken Finn's eye contact as a challenge and continued to stalk forward; its massive fangs barred. It passed the bench where he was asleep mere moments ago.

He tried to stay as still as possible, knowing that the beast could lunge at any moment and rip them apart. He smelled its strong, foul breath. Into his head popped a Psalm they had read in Sunday School: *I lie among ravenous beasts.*

Yep that's me, thought Finn. *But surely King David hadn't actually been among beasts like a hungry mountain lion.*

Finn crouched lower in the bench. He closed his eyes and instinctively did the sign of the cross, something his

Mama always told him to do when he had a bad dream.

Immediately, he heard a blood curdling scream and then more rustling.

Toni gasped. "It just left," she said in disbelief. "It let out a scream and then it turned around as if it were scared of us!"

Finn and Theodore peaked up. They were alone. Finn breathed again.

Toni hurriedly grabbed two empty suitcases and barricaded them against where the door had been.

Still in shock, the kids padded to their seats and piled extra clothes on top of them once again.

I guess the sign of the cross really does work, Finn thought as he slid down onto the bench.

"Guys," he whispered. "That mountain lion wasn't afraid of *us*. It feared something else."

"Like what?" answered Toni.

"Like the sign of the Cross that I did."

"It must have been something else," replied Theodore.

"Nuh uh. I know it. My mom always says it's a weapon against bad things," said Finn.

"Well I'm glad it worked," Toni said. "Let's get some sleep."

Finn willed sleep to come after such a crazy night. As he closed his eyes, he made a furtive sign of the Cross.

Chapter Three

"Rise and shine and give God the glory, glory!" Toni sang, nudging Finn and Theodore awake.

"As much as I love that song, I'm not in the mood," groaned Theodore.

"It's still a church trip," Toni said sarcastically, poking Finn in the ribs again.

Finn squinted as the bright sunlight poured into the bus. He yawned and moved around to crack his stiff back. Finn was also surprisingly cold last night, even with all the layers piled on him. It was crazy that the desert could be so hot and then so cold. It was like all the dramatic shifts that had happened in his life.

The Mojave Desert had long woken up. Sparrows, wrens, and mockingbirds socialized freely in the brief cool of the morning.

The three of them sat in the bus rows facing each other groggily munching on a small packet of mini Oreos.

"That was by far the scariest night of my life," said Theodore, tucking his knees to his chest.

Finn nodded absently. He didn't want to think about the ferocious cat. He wanted to bury that memory deep inside his brain, where he would never remember it.

Theodore looked between his friends, sensing that they didn't want to talk about it. "Anyways, today we need to do a full inventory of what we have," Theodore said, looking around. "We may be here for a while."

"Sounds like a plan," Toni said, brushing off brown Oreo dust. She was glad to move around and do something. Sitting around made her think about the sweltering heat that would soon engulf the bus.

The kids had pulled out all the useful supplies from the luggage yesterday, but only now took stock of what they had. With the sun quickly heating up the bus, they worked together to sort the food, clothes, and water into piles. To their dismay, the food was nothing of substance.

"We have 6 Pringle cans, 11 bags of fruit snacks, 4 big cartons of goldfish, one bag of rainbow Goldfish, 5 packets of Oreos, and 2 family sized bags of Cool Ranch Doritos. I guess it will have to do. There's an assortment of books, a couple of flashlights with no batteries, and a first aid kit. We also have 21 water bottles," Finn said, looking at the pile of supplies.

"Oh no," said Theodore, shaking his head. "We all need like half gallon a day to be comfortable and we only have—" Theodore said, checking the packaging. "2.7 gallons. The water will only last us less than two days," he said, biting his fingernail. "My dad told me about when he was doing rounds in the ER. He saw some patients who were dehydrated from like heat stroke or something. Dehydration can make you really sick, so they needed to get IVs and everything." Theodore wasn't exactly sure what an "IV" was, but he wanted to let his friends know that water was vital.

Toni looked out the bus window into the barren desert. "We have no other choice but to go look for water. Plus, we're going to need more than half a gallon each because of this heat."

"If we're going to look for water why don't we look for

the monastery?" asked Finn.

Toni nodded. "Let's try to get on top of that canyon and look around." She moved aside the suitcases she had used to barricade the doors and the three kids stepped into the desert.

Their bus had stopped in a sort of canyon, with either side of the bus closed in with sloped walls. The kids scrambled up the sandy, rocky terrain to the top. Looking around their new surroundings, Finn could only see what he was half-expecting: desert hills, a smattering of cacti, boulders, ravines. No monastery.

"I don't know if it's worth it to go look for the monastery," said Theodore glumly.

"I agree," said Toni with a sigh. "I can't see the monastery or any road or even signs of civilization."

Again, the reality of being alone in the desert sunk in.

Finn began to feel dizzy. Just standing in the mid-morning desert heat on the top of the cliff felt like being under a terrarium heat lamp.

"So then we need to find water," said Finn with finality.

They lumbered down the hill, the desert shrubs scratching against their ankles. They returned to the bus.

"We shouldn't go out now, it's way too hot," Theodore said. "We could get even more dehydrated or have heat exhaustion."

"Then we'll wait and go out tonight once it's cooler," said Finn.

"That sounds good, but it already feels like an oven in here!" Theodore said.

Finn slumped onto a seat. "Totally."

They made sure to open all the windows to get a breeze inside the stifling bus. The wind only brought warm air.

Toni returned from the back of the bus. "I've got the rainbow goldfish," said Toni in an auctioneer voice. "It's a rare one of a kind. Do I have a starting bid...?"

Finn raised his hand, laughing.

"Oh, and we have our first bid! Going once to Mr. Phineas, twice... Do you want to jump in Mr. Theodore...?"

Theodore played along and lifted his hand.

"We have Mr. Theodore in the race, going once for the man with the green shirt—oh and Mr. Phineas is back in it! Going once, going twice, sold to Mr. Phineas Mishriky!"

Finn smiled and took the packet. He opened it up and leaned across the aisle, giving Theodore a handful.

They sat on their benches once again. Toni pulled out a can of Pringles and passed it around. All the salt that they were eating dried out Finn's mouth, making him want to drink another bottle of water.

"I would give anything to just sit in a freezer and eat a whole pint of ice cream," said Theodore wistfully, sweat trickling down his back.

Finn leaned against his bench, closing his eyes. "That sounds amazing."

"We all would be sitting on the floor of a restaurant sized freezer, spooning cold and creamy goodness," Toni said, adding onto the fantasy.

"And we would have as much water as we needed,"

added Theodore.

The kids sighed.

Finn looked at their water supply. 18 bottles of water were left.

"Do you think that we should ration the water?" he asked.

"I don't think so," said Theodore, opening his eyes. "People underestimate the amount of water they need."

"Just don't guzzle it all up," said Toni, giving Theodore a look.

Finn leaned down and picked up the book he was reading on the plane. He felt a sense of comfort as he was transported into the Encyclopedia Brown book. He had gotten the entire set of books for Christmas when he was little and was rereading the series once again. Finn loved how witty the books were and how they challenged him to think of the solution before Encyclopedia Brown. The books reminded him of curling up in his bed at night and reading the books throughout the night. It almost made him forget how sweaty, exhausted, and hungry he was.

The three of them spent the afternoon reading their books, dozing off, and talking—anything to get their minds off their situation and pass the time.

By late afternoon the temperature was finally starting to cool down. Finn felt anxious again. They needed to get water.

"Let's celebrate with another dose of sugar and salt!" said Toni, raising a fruit snack.

They quickly ate dinner. Finn's stomach grumbled unhappily. The junk food was not sustainable. But he ignored it; their priority was water.

The three kids prepared for their venture into the desert. With them, they brought extra snacks, multiple bottles of water, a flashlight, and sweatshirts.

"We need something to dig to get to the water," said Finn, looking around the bus.

Toni grabbed an empty Pringle can. "Theodore give me your knife."

Theodore was a Boy Scout and always carried around his trusty knife. He was glad that he remembered to put the knife into his checked bag this time and not his backpack. Theodore had made that mistake and his previous knife was confiscated by the TSA agents.

With the shiny Swiss army knife, she expertly cut the can in half vertically. "We can use these as shovels."

The boys nodded in approval and put the shovels in the pack.

"Wait!" said Theodore. He quickly ran back into the bus and brought out the first aid kit that came in the bus. "Just in case one of you guys gets into trouble," he muttered.

"Our best chance of getting water is to dig somewhere with dense vegetation," Toni said.

Finn spotted a green smudge in the distance. "So, let's head there."

Toni scanned the horizon. "Looks to be about a mile

walk. We'll have about two hours of sunlight" she said.

With that, the three kids left the safety of the bus and ventured into the desert.

Chapter Four

"This is miserable," said Theodore. "It's like 110 degrees right now."

"Stop complaining," Toni said, checking her temperature-time-heartbeat reading watch. "It's actually only 104 degrees." She was surprised that her watch hadn't died yet.

"We've been walking for less than five minutes and you guys are already bickering like an old married couple," Finn said, laughing.

Toni smirked at Theodore, who snickered back.

"It's friendly banter," responded Toni slyly.

"We would have gotten our class schedules this week," said Theodore, avoiding a small cactus.

"I can't believe that we're going to be middle schoolers," said Finn. "All of the responsibility and no more having just one teacher."

"We're going to have seven teachers!" said Toni. "How are we going to remember them all?" she said laughing.

"I'm excited for the electives though. I signed up for chorus, so we'll see how that goes," said Theodore.

"Oh that's cool Theo," said Toni, shielding her eyes from the sun. You were one of the best singers in our Sunday School musical a couple years back."

Theodore turned red. "That was one of the most embarrassing things ever."

Theodore continued walking remembering when he had to dress up like sheep for the Nativity play. Who's ever heard of a singing sheep? thought Theodore. He was transported back to the desert when they finally arrived at the green smudge.

The "green smudge" was grand Joshua trees, vivid Chola cacti, and a mysterious cactus with spiky purple fruit. The plants decorated the bland desert with signs of life. Finn had read about almost every plant in the desert; however, he didn't recognize that weird-looking cactus.

Toni started searching the area. "Guys come help me look for moist ground," she said, leaning down and patting the ground in shaded areas.

Theodore stuck out his tongue at her back, but also began patting the ground. He had hardly slept the night before. Thoughts of desert predators, running out of food and water, and never seeing his parents again kept him from a peaceful sleep. It also didn't help that the bus's seats were poor replacements for his comfy bed.

"Let's look over here," said Finn, pointing to an especially large Joshua tree.

Toni nodded and headed to the tree.

Theodore bent down and patted the dirt. It felt like sand. "It's not even a little bit moist."

The kids continued searching the area but found nothing.

"I guess we can just try digging here," said Theodore,

going back to the Joshua tree. He didn't want to spend any more time here and get stuck in the middle of the desert at night.

Toni took one half of the Pringle can and started to shovel the loose gravel.

"We need to dig about a foot," said Toni, panting. She had dug about 6 inches in the span of a couple of minutes, working continuously.

"I can take a shift," said Theodore, trying to hide his concern. "Don't get too exhausted, I'm going to need you to carry me back," he said, cracking a smile.

Toni just wiped her sweaty brow and handed him the other half of the Pringle can. Together, they dug deeper and deeper.

"Call me when you need a break," said Finn to the others and headed to the mystery cactus a few yards away from the digging.

Finn had seen and studied his fair share of trees given that he wanted to study plants when he got older. Finn had even read books that outlined how to test if a fruit or plant was edible. When he went camping with his dad, they had tried out the method. He would have to place a little bit of the fruit on his lips, then tongue, and then slowly have a bite, making sure that he didn't have a reaction throughout the whole process. Finn grabbed one of the fruits, making sure he didn't touch a large spike.

"Ow!" Finn quickly retracted his stinging palm.

Toni stopped digging and turned around. "What happened?"

"I'm fine," he grimaced.

Toni nodded and continued shoveling.

Finn wiped off the little needles that had stuck into his palm. He didn't realize that the whole fruit was covered in not only large spikes, but also tiny needles. He quickly used the edge of his t-shirt to remove the little spikes.

"Wait, I think that's water!" yelled Theodore.

Finn ran to his friends, dropping the spiky fruit, and peered into the hole they had dug. It was just like when he dug at the beach and there was a little puddle of water when he dug deep enough. There was about an inch of water and it was slightly muddy, but it was water.

Finn high fived them and quickly regretted it. There were still a couple of translucent needles lodged in his hand.

"It's not much water," remarked Toni. "Let's wait for the water to collect a bit. What were you doing near those cacti, Finn?"

"There are little fruits on them, and I think they may be edible." He led his friends to the cacti and pointed at the fruit.

"Finn!" exclaimed Theodore. "Those are *teen shoki!* My aunt had some in her countertop fruit basket. I had never seen a fruit like that, so I picked one up. It wasn't until I had handled one for a couple of minutes, that I looked down at my hands. They were filled with tiny spikes!"

Finn nodded and showed Theodore his hands.

Theodore laughed. "You made the same mistake as me."

"Wait so can we eat them?" asked Toni.

"Yeah, they're really good, I think they're called prickly pears in English," Theodore said, carefully picking one up with his shirt.

They used Theodore's small Swiss army knife to remove all the spikes, peel the skin, and cut it up. When they cut the fruit open, beet-red juices gushed out and onto their fingers.

Finn sunk his teeth into the succulent fruit. The fresh juices oozed from his mouth and splattered his shirt. "It's kind of sour, but this beats Pringles and Doritos."

Toni and Theodore nodded in agreement as the three kids feasted on the fruit in the shade. Finn felt more energized sitting in the shade, his body growing stronger after eating something that wasn't junk food.

"I never thought I would say this, but if we get home, I'm never having chips again," said Finn, biting into another pear.

The kids got quiet.

If.

The word hung in the air, taunting them. Would they ever get home?

Finn was suddenly pulled out of his thoughts. He felt a razor-sharp pain against his thigh.

"OW! OW!"

Chapter Five

"What is it?" asked Toni, alarmed.

"I don't know." Finn spoke with difficulty. He looked around. Then he saw it. A scorpion.

"Guys! It was a scorpion! I got stung." His last words slurred slightly. He felt like his leg was about to fall off. His stomach began to cramp, and he leaned over to throw up. His head spun and he threw up again, aiming badly. Vomit splattered next to him.

Toni sprang into action. "Theo! Put him on his side. I don't want him to choke on his throw up. It was probably a venomous scorpion or something." She then located the black, shiny scorpion, who had scuttled under a rock, picked up the rock, and smashed it several times before it twitched and died.

Finn's vision began to blur. All he could see was the figure of Theodore hovering over him and Toni smashing...

As Toni dropped her rock dripping with scorpion goo, she mumbled: "He gave us the authority to trample on serpents and scorpions."

"What?" asked Theodore, looking up from Finn.

"I don't know, it just tumbled out. I think I said, 'He gave us the authority to trample on serpents and scorpions.'"

Before they could ponder what Toni said, Finn started groaning again. All he could see was stars.

"Oh no. He's throwing up more and his leg is swelling." said Theodore. Theodore's face was as white as the bleached pebbles scuffing their shoes.

"Okay, you're the medical expert. What do we do?" asked Toni. "Do you have that first aid kit?"

"I don't know if that'll help. Scorpion stings aren't common in Virginia!" he said panicking. "He needs anti-venom or something."

Finn strained to hear what else they were saying, but he felt himself starting to black out.

"Elevate the legs," he heard Theodore say, but distantly. "He's not responding!" panic rising in his voice.

"I'll run to the bus. I can make it there and back in 15 minutes." Toni said.

"There's nothing in there that will help him," Theodore whispered.

It felt like his friends were miles away. Then, he couldn't hear anything at all.

Everything went black.

He was drifting in a black void. He tried to open his eyes; he strained to hear. He couldn't. But then he heard a melodic voice.

"My dear Finn, do not worry."

Had he just died? "Uhh hello? Is someone speaking to me?" His thoughts echoed through his head.

"Hi Finn, I am Hilaria."

The name sounded familiar. Finn suddenly recognized she was one of the saints whose icon was on the bracelet his mom would make him wear.

"Hi?" Finn wasn't sure how to respond to a saint, although she sounded about his age, almost like his friend Anne from school, whose voice sounded soft and sweet. "Can you help me? I think I might die from this scorpion sting. From the looks of it I'm pretty sure it was a stripe-tailed scorpion. We're also stranded in the desert and we don't have medical supplies and we don't have a lot of water or food. Please help." The scariness of their situation washed over Finn and he started to think that none of them would make it out alive.

"Oh Finn, do not be afraid. God gives the authority to trample on serpents and scorpions, and all the powers of the enemy. Trust in the Lord with all your heart and do not lean on your own understanding."

Finn immediately began to recall the Thanksgiving Prayer he had been taught to pray daily, all his life. As if she could read his mind, Saint Hilaria proceeded to share more information about herself.

"When I was young, I left my palace to live in the desert as a monk—"

"Wait, you're a princess?" Finn was surprised. He thought saints were wise old men who looked like the priests at his church. His leg made a painful throb. He was immediately reminded of the sting. It mercifully ebbed away as his thoughts returned to Saint Hilaria.

"I was. I didn't like it though. I wanted to be a monk. The

life of prayer, fasting, and solitude appealed to me greatly, even when I was a little princess. I decided to become a monk after I heard through specific readings in the Liturgy that my calling was for Christ, to abandon my life of luxury. You see, Finn, I had an initial feeling to be a monk, but God confirmed a feeling into a calling. You will discover your calling too. I boarded a ship dressed as an important servant of the emperor and commanded it to sail for Alexandria, Egypt. The ship's captain obeyed because it seemed like I had an important message to deliver, and because I looked like a young man. I wanted to go to Egypt specifically so I could live in the Egyptian desert as a monk."

"This is really great Saint Hilaria, but I got stung by a scorpion and my friends are freaking out and I read somewhere that you die pretty soon after you get stung by a venomous scorpion." Finn just wanted to awake from the blackness.

Finn sensed her smile.

"Aren't you a kid?" The silence made Finn feel uncomfortable so he continued to elaborate on his question: "I always wondered if heaven was just filled with old people."

Saint Hilaria replied warmly, "The spirits of those who are in heaven appear of similar 'age' as when they departed. Each person's spirit takes the form of its body of the flesh, but brighter, more illumniated, and more beautiful."

As Finn began to think about his own potential for departing this life because of the scorpion's sting, the pain became more noticable. "May you help me please—I just want to get better and go back to my friends. Do you know what they're doing now?"

"They're actually praying the Thanksgiving Prayer."

"Really?" Finn didn't think his friends would do something like that. He thought Toni would try to suck the venom out of him or something and Theodore would try CPR.

"Yes. I suggested that they should."

Finn, thinking Saint Hilaria was going to continue sharing her life story, quickly interjected, "I was wondering if you could heal me as you tell your story."

"The Lord heals."

"What? I thought you were a saint!"

"What power do I have that I have not received from the true Power above. I shall pray to my kind and merciful Christ to heal who, and by His power allow you to overcome the scorpion's sting."

"Okay, Saint Hilaria, I do want to know more about your story. I will even look it up in the Synaxarion the first chance I get. But I think my friends are really worried..."

"Peace be with you Finn! See you some other time. I will be watching, even if you are not able to see me. Keep God on your mind, especially as you face troubles in the desert. The desert is a place of struggle, but also of growth. When something difficult happens to you, and you turn to God, you will take leaps and bounds in your path towards union with Him. Cast all your care upon Him, for He cares for you."

"Thanks a lot Saint Hilaria. Do you have any advice for the actual desert, not just the spiritual one?"

As Saint Hilaria's voice began to fade, she left Finn with

this last bit of advice: "Make a circle of crosses in the sand around you, and God will protect you from all the beasts of the desert."

"Okay—" Before Finn could thank her again, he was pulled from the blackness.

Chapter Six

"Lord Jesus, please help our friend, for You have covered us, helped us and guarded us—"

"Look—Finn's moving his hand!"

Theodore had been sitting next to Finn with his face buried in his hands. He jumped up in a hurry and nearly tripped over a fist-sized rock.

"Hey, Finn! Can you hear us?" said Theodore.

Toni shook Finn vigorously, who was still splayed on the ground. Finn let out a low moan.

"Oh my gosh what if he dies?!"

"Then do something, Theodore!" yelled Toni.

"Like I told you just because my dad is an ER doctor doesn't mean I know everything about scorpion stings!"

Toni let out a half-cry. "Let's give him some of this water then," said Toni. She gently poured water into Finn's half-open mouth.

They only had a sip of warm water left.

Finn started to make gurgling sounds.

"Oh no! Let's prop him up. The water probably went down the wrong pipe."

"You're going to kill him!" While Toni tried to place Finn into a sitting position, Theodore rummaged desperately through the little first aid kit. Finn flopped over again.

"I've got it. Ammonia Inhalants: Chemicals to revive a fainted person," he read from the information panel.

"Give 'em here. We've got to work fast." Toni moved the chemicals back and forth under Finn's nose. Nothing happened, except that Finn drooled a little.

As Finn lay limp on the ground, Theodore and Toni tried everything in the first aid kit to wake him. Toni even placed band aids on Finn's wispy-haired legs, and then ripped them off.

"Toni, Finn only started stirring after we prayed part of the Thanksgiving Prayer. Like right at the part of 'He gave us the authority to trample on serpents and scorpions,'" said Theodore.

"Dude, it's so random that the prayer popped into my head. I had no idea that it was going to do anything."

"Well, it did something."

"Fine. Let's try it again." In unison, Toni and Theodore began the Thanksgiving Prayer. They felt like they had no other options, and the first time they did it, Finn stirred, if only just a little. They shut their eyes hard in concentration, willing Finn to wake up.

Let us give thanks unto the beneficent and merciful God, the Father of our Lord God and Savior, Jesus Christ, for He has covered us, helped us, guarded us, accepted us unto Him, spared us, supported us, and brought us to this hour. Let us also ask Him, the Lord our God, the Almighty, to guard us in all peace this holy day and all the days of our life.

Please God let him live, let him live, thought Theodore.

Without any medical supplies or hospitals around, he knew this was all they could do.

O Master, Lord, God the Almighty, the Father of our Lord, God and Savior, Jesus Christ, we thank You for every condition, concerning every condition, and in every condition, for You have covered us, helped us, guarded us, accepted us unto You, spared us, supported us, and brought us to this hour.

God, wake up Finn. Please, thought Toni as she prayed. The Thanksgiving Prayer rolled effortlessly off her tongue. She was glad that she was required to memorize it in third grade.

Therefore, we ask and entreat Your goodness, O Lover of mankind, to grant us to complete this holy day, and all the days of our life, in all peace with Your fear. All envy, all temptation, all the work of Satan, the counsel of wicked men, and the rising up of enemies, hidden and manifest, take them away from us, and from all Your people, and from this holy place that is Yours.

But those things which are good and profitable do provide for us; for it is You Who have given us the authority to tread on serpents and scorpions, and—

"—upon all the power of the enemies," croaked a voice.

"What was that?!" Toni and Theodore's eyes popped open and looked down in astonishment as Finn was trying to get up.

"Finn! You're okay!" said Theodore.

"Don't waste your energy jumping around, Theodore." Toni sent Theodore a look. She was so relieved she could cry but didn't want the boys to see her tears. They needed her to be tough.

She then turned to Finn, her voice cracking slightly from the heightened emotions she felt only a few moments before. "I'm glad you're back Finn. What happened? Theodore told me that people stung by scorpions die, like right away."

"Umm... it was kind of crazy." Finn coughed a few times before continuing. He tried standing up.

"Sit down, Finn! You just survived a scorpion sting!" Toni pushed him back into a sitting position a little roughly.

"Thanks, Toni," said Finn with a wan smile. She always found a way to be so caring to the point that it hurt. "Do we have any more water? Getting stung by a deadly scorpion is kinda dehydrating."

"No. That's what we need to continue doing—finding water. We all need it. It's a good thing we have some in the bus. Finn, if you're able to, we need to walk the mile to the bus to rehydrate. This 'oasis' was a dud," said Toni

"Yeah, I think I can make it, but I have to tell you guys about what happened when I was out. I think a saint visited me or something." Finn's voice was still raspy, and the effort to speak made his heart race.

"Wait really?" said Theo.

"Let's talk on the way back to the bus, it's getting late and I don't want to get caught in the dark." Toni put up her right hand to the horizon, extending her arm, and pointing her fingers to the right between the horizon and the sun. She muttered, "Three fingers in between the ground and the sun... we have about 45 minutes until nightfall," she said aloud.

The kids trudged the mile back using the crooked Joshua trees that dotted the desert as landmarks. They were all so parched, but there was nothing left to drink. They had wasted precious time, water, and energy looking for water, without getting any in return.

The kids listened as Finn recounted the story of Saint Hilaria speaking to him, but both Toni and Theo secretly agreed that this was a product of the scorpion venom in Finn's veins. They didn't believe that saints could "visit" people, let alone scraggly kids in the desert. He must have imagined it all.

Toni thought over what had happened. She had never been in a situation where someone was this close to... dying. She shuddered. She knew she had to act tough and indifferent—Theodore would freak out even more if she wasn't strong. But secretly, she was on the verge of tears of relief. Losing Finn would be... no, she couldn't even name how terrible it would be. Looking down at Finn, who was leaning against her, she felt a newfound appreciation for Finn and his kindness and level-headedness.

Theodore looked out at Finn and Toni walking ahead of him. He felt like a failure. Toni was relying on him to know how to take care of Finn. He always prided himself on knowing more about medicine than others his age, but he had to realize his shortcomings. Just because his dad was a doctor and Theodore loved learning about medicine, didn't mean he should pretend to know everything. And his pride could have cost them Finn's life.

With knowing looks, Toni and Theodore helped Finn back to the bus. Finn was burnt, exhausted, and thirsty but he knew he was lucky to be alive. No, not just lucky, he was blessed. He had a saint looking after him.

Chapter Seven

With Toni helping Finn along, the kids made it to the bus before sunset. They collapsed into the bus, utterly exhausted. They were all drenched in sweat, covered in dirt, and burnt all over except where their shorts and shirts protected them. The kids eagerly drank a water bottle each—water had never tasted so good.

Finn trembled slightly as he sat down on his bench. "I am never sitting on the ground again," he muttered.

Theodore and Toni gave each other knowing looks. Their friend had been pushed to his physical, emotional, and mental limits when he got stung by the scorpion.

"It's okay, Finn," said Theodore, giving him a pat on his shoulder. "Let's get some rest," he said, wrapping a sweatshirt over himself.

"And we don't need to sit when we're out in the desert. We can stand," said Toni, trying to make Finn smile.

The three kids curled up on their benches and tried to get some rest.

"Psst. Toni! Can you hand me some goldfish?" Theodore whispered to Toni, who was falling asleep next to the food.

"Go eat a cactus," murmured Toni, who clearly didn't want to get up. She peered down at her watch. "It's already 9:00 pm, go to bed."

Theodore grumbled. He leaned over the aisle and grabbed the crispy. He munched quietly on his snack, but his stomach's growling betrayed his obvious hunger. Soon however, both Theodore and Toni were fast asleep, the stress and activity from the day washing over them.

Finn couldn't sleep, but not from hunger. Yes, the food that they had eaten in the past two days was pitiful, but it was thoughts about Saint Hilaria that was keeping him up. Why had she visited? And why had she helped him? He didn't like church that much except for the pizza they would provide after Liturgy and for seeing his friends. He wasn't crazy about the Coptic language like Mina, who loved serving as a chanter, or hymns, like Mary, who always sang the loudest. How could a saint visit him? He wasn't special.

His thoughts drifted to the events of the day. The walk from the bus to the desert, finding the prickly pairs… getting stung. He felt a sudden pain in his thigh. Finn sat up; all was dark and quiet as he grabbed his leg. He looked quickly around, making sure no scorpions had wandered into the bus to sting him. He strained to see underneath in the dark as he pushed aside the hoodies piled up as blankets. Then the pain ebbed away.

"I was just imagining it," whispered Finn. A lone tear escaped down his face. He cried because he couldn't believe the situation he was in. He cried because he wanted to go back home. He cried because he wanted this to be over.

"Finn, don't cry."

"Saint Hilaria! Is that you?" He was actually happy to hear from her. Even though he couldn't see her, he imagined a jovial girl with an endearing presence.

"Yes, yes, it's just me. Don't worry, Finn, really. You don't know who is on your side. Since I saw you, you have wanted to handle everything on your own. But you can't. You have a Father in Heaven who is there for you, every single second. Not even a scorpion sting or being lost in the desert is scary if the Creator of all deserts and all scorpions is looking after you. I've really, really been wanting to tell you what you're missing. With God in your life, you will have someone who always looks after you and cares for you. He has armies of angels and is the Lord of Hosts. Just look!"

Finn felt as if everything had become clear. He peered out of the bus window into the silent, dark night to suddenly see forms of light surrounding the bus. They were everywhere. Near that Joshua Tree! And next to the hood of the bus! Everywhere, he felt the power of these beings. And they were all standing ready to heed the command of God to guard and serve all who will inherit salvation.

"Do you see now?"

"Yes, Saint Hilaria. I see them," said Finn in a hushed voice. He turned his head to look around to the other side, and there were more holy angels.

"Finn, it is so important that you let God into your life. You have been very apathetic towards leading a spiritual life."

"Apathetic?"

"It means you don't care. You don't hate church; you just don't care about it very much."

Finn thought about this. He guessed that she was right, he didn't care about spiritual stuff.

"Isn't everyone like that?" He thought at least his friends were 'apathetic.'

"Your friends are all different. I'll send some of my friends to speak to them. Worry about yourself first, and then you can help your friends lead a more God-fearing life."

"Okay."

"I want this to be a wakeup call for you. You are loved, Finn, and I don't want you to stray further from the source of all joy and peace," continued Saint Hilaria.

"When you are scared, or tired, or even happy, thank God, talk to Him, read about the holy saints as examples for your life. During my life on earth, I was faced with many uncertainties and troublesome matters; and by prayer and trust in God, I was able to live a blessed life in the desert. I faced hardships when I left my family and when I had trouble hiding my identity. But that never conquered me. In the book of Romans, it says, 'If God is for us, who can be against us?' Remember that verse."

"Saint Hilaria … thank you for being here with me. Why did you come for a person who doesn't really care about loving God?" Finn struggled to wrap his mind around the fact that this amazing woman–this saint, was looking after him.

"Thank God in all things. It's not me, it's the God of love and compassion. I'm here because all the way in Virginia, your mom and dad are praying for you and your friends' safety and have asked me to pray to the Lord for all of you."

Finn felt tears well up. He hadn't thought much of his

parents in the craziness of the past few days. He missed them. He missed how his mom liked listening to church praises—*tasbeha*—while she cooked tacos after a long day of work in D.C or how his dad always sang off-key in church, even when Finn told him to quiet down.

A tear dripped down his nose. *I shouldn't cry, I'll dehydrate myself.*

"Finn, your parents are fine. Please don't worry. Remember, God is your refuge. He is always, always there when you are sad or alone or confused. He guided me through so many troubles, like when my sister was possessed by an evil spirit. I didn't know what to do, but when I prayed and fasted, my sister was healed. When I was sad and overwhelmed, God calmed me and gave me peace."

Finn nodded slowly and breathed through his mouth because his nose had gotten all stuffy from crying. "Saint Hilaria, can you help me? I want to turn to God just like you did when you became a monk. I want you to be my heavenly friend I can count on to pray for me. Can you please comfort my parents? Can you tell them I'm okay?"

"Yes, Finn. Go to sleep. Pray to God and remember that He is with you," she said, her voice fading away.

Finn felt utterly alone … *Wait. Why do I feel this way? I'm not alone!* Finn remembered the wise words of Saint Hilaria: "He is always there when you are sad or alone …"

Finn sat up a little in his nest of spare clothes to send a silent prayer: *Dear God, thank You for always being with me and for sending me Saint Hilaria. She's awesome. Let her be my intercessor and friend. Please Lord, help me to sleep well and to keep me and my friends safe. Please be with my parents and keep any scorpions away. In Christ Jesus, our Lord, and through the prayers of Saint Hilaria, Amen.*

Finn desperately wanted to tell Toni and Theodore about what happened but couldn't muster the energy to wake them up. With that, Finn drifted off into a deep, dreamless sleep.

Chapter Eight

Finn woke to desert sunshine filtering into the bus. Outside, he could see mist rising up against imposing mountains and birds flitting from one cactus to another. It was beautiful. After two nights of sleeping in the bus, he was surprised that he had gotten somewhat used to the hard benches.

"Guys, wake up," said Finn. He propped himself onto his elbow to see if the others had woken up.

"Beat you to it," Toni said from the back of the bus. She was already helping herself to a bag of fruit snacks. "I wish we had brought back some of those *teen shoki*. I miss fresh food." She looked down at the slightly squished, fruit-shaped gummies with a frown. "Oh well, we got to eat something." Toni then proceeded to poke Theodore in the stomach. His glasses were skewed into an awkward position on his face, and he seemed to be fast asleep. "Wakie wakie little baby!"

Theodore shifted on the bench so his back was to Toni. "Why are you the one always waking me up? I bet Finn could wake me up more gently," he grumbled, his eyes still shut. With a sigh, Theodore removed his glasses to rub his eyes. "I had a really weird dream last night about a saint."

"Wait, what?" Toni looked shocked. "I also had a dream about a saint. Her name is Saint Barbara. She told me about her life, and you should definitely hear this because it's crazy." The boys looked up with full attention, confusion and surprise evident on their faces. Toni took a big breath and readied herself to tell the story. Her eyes shone as she began. "Okay, so Saint Barbara's father wasn't Christian, and he locked her away in a tower to 'protect her from harm,'" she said in air quotes. "That's like bad parenting on a whole new level—Rapunzel style," she said, popping another gummy.

"When she told her father that she was a Christian and didn't want to get married, he sent her to be tortured. But, and I can't believe this, she was so strong in her faith during all the bad stuff she endured.

"She eventually died for Christ because people hated her for following Him. I can't imagine being okay with people who hate me for believing in God. She explained to me how going to church and telling God about all the things that make me angry will make me less upset. I never thought of turning to God in that way. You know, I want to be more patient like Saint Barbara. She's an amazing person and it was so cool to hear from an actual saint."

"I mean she also sounds awesome," said Finn. "It's crazy that I've never heard of her, just like I had never heard of Saint Hilaria. And it's crazy that her own dad sent her to be tortured," he remarked with a shiver.

"Don't worry. He was later struck by lightning and reduced to ashes," said Toni, nonchalantly.

Theodore gaped. "Okay that was a pretty cool saint story, but I think the saint that visited me has an even cooler story," he said, leaning across the aisle and grabbing a packet of fruit snacks.

"Let's hear the story then," said Toni.

"It was Saint Macrina who visited me," said Theodore.

"Her entire family was saints—like all her siblings, her parents, and her grandparents. She lived as a nun after her fiancé died and influenced her younger siblings, who would become the Saints Basil the Great, Gregory of Nyssa, and Peter of Sebaste. She was their teacher and looked after them, making sure they knew and lived the Christian life. She was also very devoted to her mother, and the two of them converted their house into a monastery. You know how she looked after her siblings? Well when the people of their area nominated Saint Gregory to be a bishop, he didn't want to do it. But when his sister encouraged him and reminded him that he had the skills to lead the church, he agreed. Saint Macrina wasn't a martyr and didn't live in the desert, but she had a huge influence on the Church through her family."

Toni conceded a smile. "She sounds pretty incredible too. Imagine being the older sister to a bunch of saints. My little brothers are tiny minions whose main goal is to annoy and tackle me at every hour of the day," she said laughing.

Theodore burst out laughing. "Well I don't have three little minions, but Rebecca can be just as annoying."

"She's eight years old! At least she is somewhat mature and civil. Mark, Daniel, and Joseph surprise attack me in Nerf battles and shoot me all the time. Of course, I wrestle them to the floor and don't relent until they beg for mercy," she said grinning. "Or mom yells at me for abusing little kids and Dad warns me of injuring my pitching arm."

Finn laughed along with them. He loved seeing Toni's little brothers dressed up in suits and ties at church, and Rebecca, Theodore's little sister, running around with her friends in the church hallways. However, Finn secretly resented his friends for having siblings as built-in friends, however annoying they may be. Growing up, Finn had to rely on keeping himself entertained while his mom worked constantly. After school, he loved playing with the neighborhood kids; they biked, fished, and sledded. Of course, he also had his old dog Nacho, a chihuahua and pug mix, who slept most of the day and never ran unless it was time for a car ride.

"Do you believe me now about Saint Hilaria? You guys thought I was making stuff up because of the scorpion venom," said Finn. He raised an eyebrow.

"Sorry, Finn we believe you now," said Theodore meekly.

"Yeah, yeah, I knew you were onto something then," harrumphed Toni.

Finn just grinned as his friends shifted uncomfortably.

"Anyways, it's so weird. Here we are, stuck in the desert, with almost no water left, and now, we hear the voices of saints in our dreams," said Finn.

"I guess that even in the desert all alone without our parents, we're being watched over. And maybe we were always watched over, but we're only now realizing it," said Toni.

"Yeah, and we can use their stories as an example. Like how to be patient … Or courageous, and … caring about others," said Theodore.

"Even though these saints are so cool, they were just like us at one point," Toni said.

"Stuck in the desert?" said Finn with a laugh.

"No, real humans who laughed and ate and made

mistakes," she said as she got up and searched through their stash of water bottles. All were empty except one—they had followed Theodore's advice and had kept well hydrated. "This is what we need to work on today," she said. "It's like 95 degrees already and this water is not going to last."

"I say we drink it now, and then go look for more water," said Finn. The kids looked out into the desert. Heat waves lazily shimmered up off the ground, and there were no birds nor animals in sight. The barren desert made Finn shiver. If they didn't succeed in finding water, they wouldn't have anything to come back to.

"Are you sure we can travel out there? Why don't we stay in the shade of the bus until it gets cooler? Maybe we can play cards and then take a nap," said Theodore, who shuddered at the idea of walking more than ten minutes in the scorching heat. The sunburn on his face still hurt. He had never wanted sunscreen so bad.

"I just want to distract myself," said Toni. "And maybe we can share more about our saint friends."

They all agreed. Thinking about the heat, his thirst, and all the saints made Finn's brain spin. He just needed a break.

The kids settled down on the benches and broke out a deck of cards. Using spare pencils they found in the luggage, they played an intense game of spoons.

"I'm still so shocked at how all this has happened to us," said Toni as she dealt cards at a furious rate.

"When they talk about saints at church, they don't seem like real people," Finn struggled to put words to his thoughts. "Like, the only girl saint anyone really mentions in Liturgy is Saint Mary. And any other saint doesn't seem to have a, an umm—" he broke off, unsure of how to continue. "They don't seem to have a personality," he finished.

"I agree. But now that *actual* saints have talked to us, I realize that they are so cool. Saint Macrina is like my old Sunday School teacher—she's so kind and caring and strong. I want Saint Macrina to be my intercessor always," said Theodore.

They played in silence for a moment.

"And our saints are best friends with Jesus. I want that too," said Toni in an almost whisper. None of her favorite athletes or Broadway stars or historical figures could compete against Orthodox saints. Their love for Christ made them super celebrities, and the thing was, none of them actively looked for fame or praise. Saint Barbara was so humble, even though she knew that her dad and his cronies were wrong. *Saint Barbara, I want to be humble like you are.* She sent a silent prayer just as she silently grabbed a pencil from the Spoons pile.

As the cards were going around and around, Finn thought about when the three of them had first met.

Finn had just moved to Northern Virginia from Minnesota and was attending Saint Mark's Church for the first time. His mom had just been appointed head of the Fish and Wildlife Service. She would now be working in D.C. while his dad stayed at home. He was glad because he was a great cook—his kofta kebabs were to die for. Finn was sad to leave Minnesota. He would miss visiting Mall of

America or eating brunch at Perkins with his grandparents.

After the Liturgy, he was guided up the stairs to the first grade Sunday School room. Kids were sitting around small tables coloring and laughing. When Finn sheepishly entered the room, all of them immediately stopped chattering and turned to look up at him. There were hardly ever new kids in Sunday School, let alone a boy with pale skin and light hair.

Finn curled up inside. His dad was fully Egyptian, but his mom was American, and he didn't look like the other kids with their dark hair.

"Stop staring at him, Steven," yelled a voice from across the room. A stocky girl with long black hair stepped in front of him. She towered over him. "Hey, who are you?"

"Come on Toni, be nice," said a skinny boy with curly hair. "What's your name?" he asked, coming up to them.

"My name is Phineas, but I go by Finn," squeaked Finn. He was grateful for the two kids talking to him.

"The lesson hasn't started so you can come color with us," said Toni. "Theo, go get Finn some crayons."

With that, Finn, Theodore, and Toni banded together to become the best of friends.

The kids had never played as much Spoons as they had that morning. Both Finn and Theodore were knocked out, leaving Toni the winner. After the game, the three kids settled onto their respective benches to sleep away the hottest part of the day. The topic of their dreams? Water.

Chapter Nine

"What are you looking for?" Finn's question came out like a series of frog croaks.

"Water," Toni's voice also sounded crackly and strained. "We don't have any left, but I'm doing another search."

Outside, the desert began to stir in the absence of the heat. Jackrabbits with comically long ears peeped out from bushes where they sheltered from the Mojave sun. Red-tailed hawks patrolled the skies for a quick meal.

"We've got to look for more. I felt like all the water got sucked from me during that nap."

Finn nodded in agreement.

"Let's go scouting. There might be an oasis with a natural spring," said Toni. "I'm going to wake up Theodore."

Before she could clap her hands loudly next to his sleeping body, Finn stepped in between and gently shook Theodore awake.

"I guess I shouldn't do that," Toni said with a wry smile. "Saint Barbara wouldn't."

With all three kids awake, they began charting out where to search for water.

"Okay so we went that way for our first try," said Toni pointing to the left of the bus.

"So let's try the other way," said Theodore.

"We could search the entire desert and not find anything. I wish I could just call Saint Hilaria or something and ask for help," sighed Finn.

"Isn't that like prayer? Asking for help?" Theodore said. "We could try praying."

"Yeah I guess we can try. Saint Barbara always did that when she was happy or when she was in trouble," said Toni, who very much wanted to be like the fierce Saint.

They all looked around a bit awkwardly, but at Toni's insistence, they all stood up to pray outside the bus.

"Um, dear God, thank you for being with us in the desert. We really need Your help and Your comfort. Right now, we're out of water. Please guide us and be with us when we search for water. And please help us find water. In Christ Jesus and through the prayers of Saint Hilaria, Saint Barbara, and Saint Macrina. Amen," prayed Finn shyly.

He never liked praying in front of other people and would look away when a Sunday School teacher needed someone to pray. But now, in their time of need, Finn felt comforted by this prayer. It made him feel less anxious about not having enough water.

"That made me feel better," said Theodore.

"Finn! Your bracelet is glowing!" yelled Toni.

Finn looked down to see his wooden bracelet with saint icons glowing faintly, as if it were glow-in-the-dark. Except it was daytime.

"Take it off! Maybe it's a chemical reaction!" said Theodore, who had taken two steps back.

"I can't! It's stuck or something." Finn wiggled the

bracelet back and forth. But it was no use. It was like it had latched onto his wrist.

Toni grabbed his arm. "Let me see if I can get it off." She tugged, but it only seemed to tighten around Finn's wrist.

"Wait!" exclaimed Theodore as Toni tried to get the bracelet off. She had pulled Finn away from the bus and the bracelet had glowed brighter.

"Hold on. Toni, move Finn more towards the right," instructed Theodore. Toni obeyed, and the bracelet again glowed brighter.

"Let's try going in the bus—it might just be a trick of the light," said Finn, rubbing his eyes with the other hand. The kids tramped back into the hot bus, and as they did, the glowing grew faint. By the time they were near their "beds" at the back of the bus, they could hardly see any light coming from the bracelet.

"The glowing changes as Finn moves," said Theodore in a voice full of confusion and awe.

"He's right, let's move Finn over here," Toni walked Finn down the aisle closer to the bus door. Finn shuffled along with Toni—his eyes never left the bracelet.

Theodore was right; the bracelet's brightness changed as Finn moved closer or farther from the bus.

"It's obviously brighter when we go that way," said Toni, pointing to the right. "How about we walk that way? Who knows, it might be a sign that we should go there," she said, looking closely at the saints on Finn's bracelet.

"Hold on, is that Saint Barbara on the bracelet? It says so right there! Oh and that icon says Saint Hilaria!" said

Toni.

"And that's Saint Macrina!" said Theodore.

The kids stopped walking and peered closely at the bracelet.

Toni looked up sharply to Finn. "It was the prayer," she whispered.

The kids stood in silence, taking in the fact that this bracelet might be glowing because of a prayer.

"It means God and His Saints are helping us," said Theodore in a hushed voice. In their silence, the symphony of bird calls continued, oblivious to the children's revelations.

Finn looked down at the bracelet, which, because they were outside and to the right of the bus, was bright in the afternoon light. "Let's go wherever the bracelet continues to glow brighter," he said definitively.

"It might lead us to water, or even rescue," chimed Theodore, whose eyes still fixated on the bracelet.

With Finn leading the way, the kids wound their way past shrubs and sand and rocks, over a large hill, and down a small valley.

"Do you remember that time when the water fountain broke outside our Sunday School classroom? I always used it after Liturgy and the time it broke, I really needed water," said Theodore. "I was so thirsty, but it's nothing compared to this," he said with a low chuckle.

Finn could only nod in agreement. His tongue felt oddly swollen in his mouth, and he had a hard time focusing on the conversation. The only thoughts flickering through his mind were centered around the one thing he couldn't have—water. Finn reflected that throughout his life, he usually got what he wanted: new toys and gadgets, picking what restaurant his family went out to, soft cookies at the grocery store. He had never experienced a desperate need, certainly not a life threatening one.

Now water was all he could think about. Finn couldn't recall a time when he wanted something this bad—not even the semi-automatic-long-barreled-green-and-orange nerf gun that was now collecting dust in his closet.

As they trudged along, Finn's bracelet steadily grew brighter. It was their only comfort in the heat and thirst.

Chapter Ten

The sun sank behind the dusty hill as the kids' optimism sank to a new low. Even though the bracelet was almost blindingly bright, the kids had been out in 95°F weather for an hour. With no water. Their pace was slow over the harsh terrain and Finn was about ready to give up. By now, Toni was leading the way; she looked back every few seconds to make sure the bracelet was glowing brighter as they zigzagged through the terrain.

"I need a break after this hill," panted Finn.

"I second that," said Theodore.

The trio lumbered up a rocky hill, sparsely decorated with wind-beaten shrubs. Reaching the top, they could see for miles around them.

"Oh look! That's the bus," pointed out Toni. The bus was a small white smudge in the valley.

"Here's what we should really be looking at!" exclaimed Theodore.

The kids turned from the direction in which they came from to face the other side of the hill. Down below was a greenish-blue pool of water. It was surrounded by the lushest plants the kids had seen yet: towering palm trees and bright green shrubs and assorted cacti bearing fruit.

"It must be a mirage," whispered Toni.

"Race you to it!" All three sprinted to the oasis with

new-found energy. They neglected to notice that Finn's bracelet glowed its brightest and then suddenly stopped.

"It's real!" yelled Theodore.

They navigated around boulders and cacti to the edge of the pond.

"Can we drink this?" asked Toni, her eyes wide. She wanted to lean down and slurp up the entire pond, but she knew some water wasn't safe to drink.

"We have to. I mean, at least I will. I'm too thirsty," said Finn. He knelt down and scooped some water. "It tastes good," he said. The water was pure relief on his poor swollen, parched tongue and throat.

"Okay," said Toni cautiously. She bent down and slurped. "Come have some, Theodore!"

Theodore reluctantly drank. The trio spent the next few minutes drinking as much water as they could.

"Ah, I feel so much better," said Theodore as he wiped his wet mouth with the back of his hand.

"I'm so surprised that there's this much water!" exclaimed Toni. "My Tayta lives not too far away and she's a big activist for water conservation in desert areas."

"What do you mean by that?" asked Theodore, sipping water from his hands.

"Well, deserts hardly have any rainfall, so plants and animals have adapted to survive with little water. But people who live in the desert have to tap deep underground aquifers—they're like really big lakes deep underground. She told me that in some places, the aquifers levels have dropped more than 200 feet in the last 50 years! She especially hates golf courses. Imagine using tons and tons of gallons to make grass grow. In the desert." Toni rolled her eyes in frustration.

"So what does your Tayta do about it?" asked Theodore.

"Well, she used to be an environmental science professor at a university in Arizona. Now that she's retired, she helps local water management better conserve water and teaches kids about conserving water at school events."

"What's also interesting is that she was going to do all this in Egypt (because it's basically all desert.)

"Why didn't she?" interrupted Finn.

"Well, she said something about being both Christian and a woman equals no jobs," mused Toni.

"Wow that sucks," said Theodore.

"Yeah, so now she lives in California."

"We're so lucky to have found this place," said Finn.

"Hold up. We aren't lucky. God helped us through the bracelet! Did you forget that we would have never found this if it weren't for us asking God for help?" demanded Toni.

The boys looked down at their toes from where they were sitting in the shade of the surrounding vegetation.

"You're right, Toni," said Finn meekly.

"Of course I am. I can't believe you two thought we did this—" she gestured to the lushness of the oasis "—without help." She shook her head in disbelief.

"Then how about we pray and thank God?" Theodore said.

The kids scooched closer on a large boulder to pray.

"Dear God, thank you for bringing us here to get water. We really needed it. Thank you for keeping us safe and for being with us in the desert. Please help us get rescued soon. Amen," prayed Theodore.

"Through the prayers of Your holy and amazing saints, Saint Hilaria, Saint Barbara, and Saint Macrina, hear us when we say thankfully: Our Father…" The kids' voices rose up into the setting sun's twinkling light as birds flitted around them.

"We should probably go back now," said Toni, "It's getting dark."

The kids were still wet from playing in the little pond. The pond had formed as a result from a deep, underground spring that welled up pure water from an even deeper underground aquifer. Any other pool of water would have made the kids very sick.

They swam, played Marco Polo, and enjoyed themselves for the first time in this whole scary situation. It was also a chance to wash off all the sweat, sand, and grime that had accumulated in the past days.

"Yeah, we should," said Theodore with a sigh of regret. "I don't want to leave this place! It has water, a pool where we can swim, and water… Did I say that already?!"

Finn looked out from where they came from. "I don't want to leave either," said Finn longingly. "But we have no protection from predators. I was at the zoo one time and it said, right outside the cheetah enclosure, that a sixth-grade kid is the perfect-sized meal," he said.

"I agree. Even if cheetahs don't live here, we should get back" said Toni. She shuddered thinking about the one-eyed mountain lion prowling around at night.

"Umm, okay, but how do we get back? Was it just me, or were you all just staring at the bracelet and not paying attention?" Theodore said.

"I'm sure we can find our way back. We went over several hills and down some valleys. It shouldn't be too hard." said Toni.

They walked up the oasis basin onto a small ridge. Around them was the monochromatic desert: rocky, sandy, dry. It all looked the same.

Toni regretted her original confidence but resolved to lead the way anyway.

"Okay, we have to go this way," she said in her most confident voice.

"Are you sure? I thought we passed that Joshua Tree and went that way," said Theodore.

"Nuh-uh! We went that way," pointed Finn, farther to the right.

Toni realized none of them really knew how to get back. She had to be the first to admit that she had been wrong or else they would be walking in circles.

"Guys," she said. "I don't think any of us know where to go." She stared her steely stare at Finn and then at Theodore. "Face it. You don't know where we're going, and you don't know where we're going, and I don't know where we're going. We can't pretend. It'll get us in trouble."

She sat down in a huff. Theodore and Finn also sat down, a bit ashamed.

"What should we do then?" asked Finn.

"To be honest, I think our best bet would be to look for high ground and try to see the bus," replied Toni.

"That sounds like a plan," said Theodore, who looked nervously at the sinking sun.

With that, the kids shouldered their backpacks, now lighter from snacks eaten, and set off for high ground.

Finn could still feel the embarrassment he felt when Toni called him out for pretending to know how to get home. *Why did I pretend?* He navigated around scruffy shrubs as he reflected. Maybe he wanted to be a hero for his friends. *I can't think like that. I could have led them the wrong way.* He climbed up a steep hill littered with unstable rocks and looked out from the top. In the dusk to the left, he could see a smudge of white.

"I see the bus!" said Finn.

"Me too!" said Toni and Theodore at the same time.

"Jinx! You owe me a—" Toni paused to think. "—a refreshing bottle of water!"

"Mmm I could use that right now," said Theodore.

Flushed with the excitement of seeing the bus, the three kids walked down the hill, up another hill and down to the bus. As he walked up the three steps into the bus, Theodore almost felt like he was arriving home.

"Today was awesome," said Theodore. With stomachs

full of water, the day did seem awesome.

"Thank God," said Toni.

"I just wish we had brought back some of that water," Finn said.

"That's what we'll do tomorrow. We'll take some of these empty water bottles and go back to the oasis," said Toni.

Content with their day's work and their plans for the next day, the kids nestled into their make-shift beds.

Finn heard a faint voice just before he fell into a deep sleep: "Good work today, Finn. I told you trusting in God will get you places."

Chapter Eleven

Theodore woke to the Mojave sun shining directly onto his face. He yawned and looked around. Toni and Finn were fast asleep. That was weird—usually he was the last to wake up. An idea popped into his head before he went to go to the bathroom. What if he could rudely wake up Toni like she always does to him? He tiptoed up to Toni's bench. She was drooling slightly. He stopped and remembered how much he hated it when Toni woke him up with a powerful shake. Maybe he should just let her sleep.

When he returned from outside, Toni and Finn were awake.

As usual, Toni was up and taking breakfast orders.

"We have one more Oreo packet, plenty of Pringles, and the family sized bag of Doritos," she said, holding up the options.

Theodore cringed a little. They had been eating junk food for several days. And while he always felt excited when he could eat chips at parties (they weren't allowed in his house), he couldn't stand eating more Pringles. Plus, eating was getting difficult for him—his gums were swollen and sore. Even though there were toothbrushes, they didn't want to waste water. He guessed that was because of not brushing his teeth, or maybe because he wasn't eating fruits or vegetables. His mom always told him that fruits and vegetables have nutrients and vitamins you can't get elsewhere. Especially not from Oreos.

"Let's eat quickly and then head out while it's cool," said Theodore, resigning himself to some Doritos.

Toni laughed. "You look like a marshmallow!"

"It was cold last night," Finn said. He had on several layers of sweatshirts, making him look like—he sighed—a marshmallow.

They clambered out of the bus into the early morning Mojave mist. Theodore was still not used to the beauty of the desert. It was a land of extremes. The scorching heat, the frigid cold. And in between birds and mammals and reptiles and plants thrived.

"Stuff your bag with empty water bottles," said Toni, "and then I think we can retrace our steps from yesterday." Before they headed away from their vehicular home, they said a quick prayer.

"Dear God, thank you for keeping us safe. We thank You for Your love and mercy and for watching out for us. Please keep us safe and let us reach the oasis safely. Amen."

So off they went.

"I just can't believe Andrew hasn't come back yet—I mean why would he leave us?" said Toni.

"I don't think it was his fault to leave us—he felt like that was a good idea at the time," Theodore said.

"I wonder what he's doing right now. Maybe he's

wandering the desert like us!" said Toni.

"Nuh uh. He must have gotten to safety and is now leading a search party for our rescue. I know it," said Finn, emphatically. He still felt bad about Andrew. Finn knew that Andrew only had two bottles of water and would be in trouble if he was still in the desert. He prayed a silent prayer for Andrew's safety and for their rescue.

"Wait, what's that sound?" Theodore shaded his eyes and tried to look up at the sky.

Finn could hear something too. A low buzzing sound.

"No way!" yelled Toni. "It's a plane!" She started jumping up and down, waving her arms in an effort to catch the plane's attention.

The little plane was coming closer. The kids could all hear it and see it now.

Finn took off his bright red shirt and waved it in the air. "Theo! Use your glasses as a reflection!"

Theodore yanked off his glasses and angled it so that the sun's ray would bounce into the pilot's eyes. "We need to get to the bus!" he yelled over the noise. "It's a big landmark!"

Toni sprinted to the bus that was less than 1,000 feet away. The boys ran as fast as they could but lagged behind.

"The plane is circling back! Away from the bus!" cried Finn, disappointment creeping into his voice. This may have been their one shot. "Theodore stay here and keep using your glasses. I'm going to run to the bus."

Theodore nodded and tried to catch his breath as he angled his glasses up into the bright sky. The bright reflection from the glasses would hopefully catch the pilot's attention.

The one engine plane zoomed back around towards the bus and Finn was filled with hope again. He hurtled at full speed to the bus trying to yell and wave his arms at the same time. He could see Toni on top of the bus, waving her arms frantically.

Finn could just imagine getting rescued and being taken away from this dry desert. He would be reunited with his parents and his dog Nacho. Toni would see her brothers and Theodore would see his younger sister. Maybe Saint Hilaria was behind this.

Finn snapped back to reality as the plane passed the bus. It grew smaller, and then faded away.

Finn, out of breath, sagged against the bus's steps, defeated.

Toni didn't sit down. She paced back and forth. "They should have seen the bus! Look at it! It's huge!" she raged.

Theodore stumbled to the bus. "I'm so sorry guys," he said crying. "My hands were shaky and I couldn't get the pilot's attention." He wiped his eyes, still sobbing. He sat down next to Finn who patted his back.

"It's not your fault," Finn said, trying to comfort himself and his friend.

"Why didn't God allow that plane to rescue us?" demanded Toni.

Theodore just sniffled and Finn shook his head. The three sat for a while in the shade of the bus. Toni collected herself first.

"I know we're all super disappointed, but we still need to get to the oasis! We've already used up energy and water running back to the bus. We need that water," said Toni. "Come on boys, get up."

The boys slowly got up and the three walked again in the direction of the oasis, this time, with less excitement in their step.

Toni thought of how *good* going home would be. She felt a yearning in her stomach for her parents and brothers and even her house. Her room was decorated with her softball trophies and her pottery creations. She had pictures of beaches and with her softball team. In the closet of her room hung a palm-sized icon of Saint Mary and baby Jesus, both looking stern. *Hmmm. I need to get an icon of Saint Barbara and maybe move the icon of Saint Mary and Child to a better part of my room. Right now, they're the ones looking after me, not my softball team.* Thoughts of home lingered in Toni's head as they reached the oasis and filled their water bottles up with the cool spring water.

Finn felt uneasy as they walked back to the bus. He kept thinking about the tiny plane. *It could have been a rescue plane,* he thought. Finn began wondering about his parents back home again. *Were they back home? Did they fly to California once they heard I had gone missing?* Finn could picture his mom hysterically praying and calling every single monk, priest, and nun she knew, but lost touch with throughout the years. His dad, on the other hand, would probably be furiously calling every police station in the state of California, demanding they send a search party.

Thinking about his parents made him even sadder. He kicked at the dusty stones. It was nice that it was cloudy— usually the sky was cloudless, the sun mercilessly shining. It gave the trio some shade on their walk. Farther out, Finn could see darker, angrier clouds. He hoped they wouldn't get caught in a thunderstorm—if that was even possible in the desert.

They trekked silently, across the dry riverbed, only feeling slightly better, they were almost to the bus. Finn looked down. The pebbles on the riverbed skittered around his feet.

"Guys, what is happening?" said Finn.

They then heard a rumble. Then a roar.

And then they saw it.

"Run!!" screamed Toni.

Chapter Twelve

To their left, a wall of water was rushing towards them. Not clear blue water, but murky, muddy water filled with sticks, dead branches, and other debris.

The kids turned and sprinted in the other direction.

It was no use.

They could not outrun the forces of nature.

In seconds, the water engulfed Finn and swept him up. The tide of water was cold, rushing up his nose as he flipped and tumbled. Finn felt objects hit his legs and arms as they flailed around trying to tread water.

Was that Theodore's head? It felt like hair.

Finn felt his backpack being ripped off his shoulders in the strong currents.

No, no, no. That has all the supplies.

He felt like a rerouting GPS, unable to find its way.

Which way was air? Where was the sweet precious air his lungs were now screaming to have?

Finn didn't know how long he could hold his breath. He was starting to see spots. He could feel that his body was weakening, losing strength in the vengeful current that was sweeping him to who knows where. He squinted, trying to open his eyes in the murky water. His eyes burned.

Was that a light?

Finn had a spark of hope.

That might be the sun!

He kicked as hard as he could to get to the surface. Finn's lungs were outraged, demanding oxygen. Sticks, logs, and dirt, was swirling around him, making it hard to follow the light. He was getting dizzier, but he knew that he was almost there. He made a final hard kick and propelled himself upwards.

He broke the surface. The thunderstorm's vengeful rain droplets pouring onto his face. He gulped down the clean beautiful air. The water swirled around him trying to drag him under again.

The riverbank was only five feet away, but the current tugged him away from shore. Finn tried to kick and propel his way through the churning water. He couldn't.

He was being swept away, farther, and farther from the bus. It was getting more and more difficult to tread water. Finn couldn't feel the bottom. The stars returned and got larger and larger.

Don't pass out, don't give up, he thought.

But giving up felt so easy.

He slipped under the surface.

Just as he was about to succumb to total darkness, he suddenly felt a strong arm scoop him around the waist.

Finn was pulled up to the surface. He tried to paddle along. He was too weak.

He was forcefully thrown onto the riverbank. The hot dirt was a relief to his shivering body as he coughed and coughed water.

"Need… to find… him…" the voice heaved.

There was a splash and then Finn was alone again.

Finn was sprawled on the bank, trying to catch his breath in the roaring thunderstorm. Rain fell fast and hard. He panted and tried to peer into the rushing river.

It was definitely Toni who saved me, thought Finn. *I think I saw Theo just moments ago, floating.*

Finn thought back when the three of them and their siblings went to a waterpark. Theodore was the only one who was afraid to go down the giant waterslide. He and Toni had tried all day to convince him to go down, but Theodore refused.

Oh no, thought Finn, panicked. *Theodore isn't a strong swimmer.*

Finn struggled to the edge, trying to get a glimpse into the muddy water.

Out of the corner of his eye, he saw two figures downstream.

Finn panted with exertion. He used all his energy to lift himself up. He half limped, half trotted closer to his friends who struggled in the water downstream. He slid and slipped in the newly formed mud.

"He's unconscious!" yelled Toni from the water. Theodore's eyes were closed. She tried to keep his head above the surface while also battling the currents.

"Give me your hand!" Finn yelled frantically, as he crouched down and extended his arm.

"Take Theo," she gasped. The weight of Theodore was pulling her down.

Finn hurriedly leaned forward and grasped Theodore by his legs, pulling him safety. He turned back to the water to help Toni, but she was nowhere to be found.

"Toni! Where are you?" he yelled desperately. He couldn't lose Toni. Finn almost forgot about Theodore, who was soaking wet and unconscious.

He felt like his world was falling apart.

Through the prayers of Saint Hilaria, Saint Barbra, and Saint Macrina, please God, save my friends. Please help me get through this. I can't do this on my own. My friends are the best, I don't want to lose them, not like this. Theodore is so kind, and Toni is so supportive. Help them. Amen.

"Dude what are you doing?! Go and help Theodore!" yelled a voice.

Finn whipped around. "You're alive!" Toni was dripping muddy water, but unharmed.

"Of course I'm alive dummy. I just got swept downstream a bit," she said crouching down next to Theodore. "Come over here and help!"

Finn hastily kneeled down to Theodore and checked the pulse on his neck. "There's a pulse."

"Let's turn him on his side! I think he swallowed water." Toni gently pushed Theodore on his side and water came rushing out of his mouth.

Finn nodded looking assured. "Toni, let's pray, I don't know what else to do. Dear God, please help Theodore. He doesn't deserve this. Amen."

"Dear God, please help Theodore..."

Theodore blinked and opened his eyes.

Finn and Toni sighed with relief. They had been praying for 20 minutes without ceasing, their voices hoarse and cracked with no water. Never had Finn been so entrenched in saying any prayer like he had now. Usually he mindlessly went along with it during Sunday School, or tried to come late to skip it completely.

Finn and Toni had cleared all the rocks and twigs from their area—anything to make their space more comfortable.

Theodore groggily pulled himself up and then tipped over.

Toni kneeled down to Theodore. "Dude chill," she said, pushing him back to the ground. "Don't overexert yourself."

"I need... water," he croaked, closing his eyes. He was soaking. Finn knew it was a combination of the flood water and the sweat that was beading down his forehead.

Finn and Toni looked at each other nervously.

All their supplies—the water they had just filled up, sweatshirts, and snacks—had been washed away in the flood. They had nothing left except the dirty clothes on their backs. They were completely lost in the desert, maybe miles from the bus.

Finn looked at his friend. He didn't want to say that they had lost everything. The news might make Theodore's condition worse.

Toni must have come to the same conclusion. "We'll get

some water later."

Theodore clearly drooped in disappointment. He slumped back down and drifted off into sleep.

They had used up so much energy trying to survive the flash flood caused by thunderstorms upriver. All three kids were severely dehydrated and *needed* water. Finn had to do something.

Toni pushed back Theodore's matted black hair and felt his forehead with the back of her hand. "He's burning up," she whispered to Finn. "I'm no doctor, but I can tell that he's in bad shape." Her large hazel eyes were brimming with tears.

Finn sighed and looked around. What could he do? He felt helpless. Theodore had thankfully not drowned, but now he had a severe fever. They had no medicine, water, fire, or shelter. What was he supposed to do? The three of them had faced countless challenges in the past couple of days, but this topped all of them.

"What else can we do," said Finn looking up at Toni. "We have to trust that God will get us through this. We can't depend on ourselves to get out of here, we have to trust in Him."

Toni nodded. She glanced down at Theodore who had fallen asleep, his entire body shivering. "I can't believe what just happened. It was just a wall of water coming straight at us."

"I think it was some sort of flash flood." Finn remembered the dark clouds upriver moments before they were swept up. "I didn't know they happened in the desert."

"Anyways, it's getting dark and we both need some rest,"

she said, becoming more businesslike. "I'll take the first shift." Toni started picking up rocks and moving them out of the way, to make space for Finn to lie down.

Finn opened his mouth, about to agree with her when he froze. A look of terror engulfing his face. "Toni, please don't move," pleaded Finn, looking over her shoulder.

Chapter Thirteen

Toni looked confused. "What's wrong Finn..." She slowly turned around, looking directly into the one bright eye of a mountain lion, merely a couple of feet away from her head, its yellowed teeth barred. It was the same mountain lion from the bus. "Oh. My. Gosh," she gasped.

The 200-hundred-pound beast didn't seem bothered that his prey stumbled to her feet and grabbed a rock; it kept stalking towards them, its muscles flexed, ready to pounce.

"Just take Theo and run," whispered Toni, tears streaming down her cheeks.

"I'm not leaving you," said Finn, taking a step back using his body to shield Theodore.

In a split second, the mountain lion leapt forward and slashed Toni in the forearm. His friend batted to the ground like a rag doll. Blood gushed down her arm and pooled on the hard ground, mixing with the rain and mud.

She had seen the animal lunge at her, but everything seemed foggy. Her world was spinning. Pebbles pressed sharp against her cheek. *I must be on my side. How did I get there?* she thought. Something warm seeped into her shirt. Her left forearm seared. Toni glanced up at her arm. It was completely shredded. Skin, muscle, and bone were exposed. Her head spun faster. She could vaguely sense a presence over her, something breathing down on her. It was the worst pain in her life. Toni could feel herself slipping away, an escape from the pain. "Lord Jesus help me!" she cried out.

Then everything went black.

Finn watched in horror from behind a shrub as the mountain lion sniffed his friend and then clamped down on her forearm, about to drag her off. More blood flowed onto the ground He couldn't think. What could he do? Suddenly, a blinding light appeared. Finn squinted.

Out of nowhere, a vaguely human form drew a sword and slashed the mountain lion, with a definitive whoosh. Just as quick as it appeared, the angel vanished, leaving the mountain lion unrecognizable, a tangled mass of fur and blood.

Finn was left with two unconscious friends and a slain beast.

A million thoughts raced through his head. He needed to focus and think, like he always did. *Get yourself together Finn,* he thought, stumbling to his feet. *God is with me always. I can do anything through Christ who strengthens me.*

Toni's left forearm gushed scarlet blood. The mountain lion must have hit an artery. She was as pale as the mountain lion's white stomach fur; she was losing blood rapidly. Finn quickly ripped a part of his shirt and wrapped it tightly around the wound. He had seen that on the crime show his dad watched. The cloth was soaked within seconds. He started to panic again.

"I need to stop the bleeding!" he yelled, frustrated.

He ripped off another chunk of his t-shirt and pushed down on the wound. Once again it was soaked in crimson blood within seconds. Toni's life was slipping away before his eyes.

Then he remembered. Theodore was the son of an ER doctor. He must have seen his father treat patients with similar injuries. It was his last hope. Finn raced to Theodore, who was in and out of sleep, sprawled on the hard ground. Finn leaned over him and gently shook him.

"Theo, I need you to wake up! God, I need you to wake him up! Please!" Finn was crying now, looking back and forth between his friends.

Theodore coughed and squinted up at Finn. "Finn...?" he asked uncertainly.

Finn sighed with relief. "Theo I really need your help." Finn didn't want his friend to get overwhelmed and go into shock, so he leaned on the vague side. "Toni is really hurt."

Theodore looked around confused and disoriented.

"Just tell me what to do," said Finn, looking back at Toni. He needed to move quickly. "Her forearm is bleeding bad."

Theodore blinked and tried to focus. He looked down at Finn's dirty sneakers. "Shoelace," he groaned. "Tie it above the wound tight." He was breathing quickly. "Put a stick through the string and twist very tightly. Make sure her wrist doesn't have a pulse." He slumped back down, drained from the few words he uttered.

Finn nodded. "Get some rest now," he said getting up and sprinting back to Toni who was a couple yards away.

He kneeled down next to Toni and yanked out his muddy shoelace. He held his breath as the wound kept spurting blood. Finn carefully wrapped the shoelace below her elbow, making sure it was as tight as possible. Already, he could tell the blood was slowing down. He frantically looked around for a stick. There was nothing. He could only see cacti, no Joshua trees. Then he remembered. He ran to the riverbed. The river had begun to recede from where it was; it had stopped raining. Finn hadn't realized that the rain had ceased. The polluted water now lazily went by with twigs and branches floating throughout. Finn got to his knees and carefully leaned in, snatching up a stick.

With the precious stick, he looped it in his shoelace and turned it clockwise until Toni's wound completely stopped bleeding. Finn quickly yanked off his other shoelace and tied the stick in place. He remembered what Theodore said and used two shaking fingers to check the pulse on her wrist. He felt nothing. He tore off another piece of his shirt and replaced it with the fresh material. He cautiously picked up the used bandage and threw it into the riverbed, he didn't want any more creatures coming around. Finn slumped back in relief. He knew Toni was still in danger, but at least the bleeding had stopped.

Finn was breathing hard. He was covered in blood, water, and sweat. His head was pounding and he was overcome with nausea. Finn was about to curl up next to his injured friends when he paused.

He just remembered something that Saint Hilaria had told him the first time she appeared. She had told him that in the dirt, he should make a circle of crosses to protect them when they're sleeping. As exhausted as he was, he got up and made a circle of crosses, big enough for the three of them to lay down comfortably. He stepped back into the circle and wiped his dusty hands on his shorts.

He pushed a rock into the circle and carefully elevated Toni's arm. Finn then positioned the three of them into a row to conserve body heat. Without a fire, they would freeze. Knowing that Toni was unconscious, and that Theodore was plagued with a severe fever, Finn decided to stay up and watch over them.

"God, please help us tonight," whispered Finn into the dark.

Finn tried to not think about the snakes, scorpions, and mountain lions that lurked around in the night. They were completely vulnerable. He envisioned the circle of crosses as an impervious shield that would protect them from any harm. He shivered and huddled closer to Theodore, as the moon shone bright above them. Finn turned on his side and looked out into the sky. He had never seen so many stars. Some were big and bright, while others were small and twinkled. In his backyard he could see stars, but nothing like this. Out here, there were no lights to pollute the sky. Seeing the wonders that God designed helped him calm down. He vowed that he would be alert throughout the night.

Chapter Fourteen

They wandered in the desert in the desolate way; They found no city to dwell in. Hungry and thirsty, their soul fainted in them. Then they cried out to the Lord in their trouble, and He delivered them out of their distresses. (Psalm 107:4-7)

"Finn! Finn wake up!"

He awoke to someone jabbing his back.

"There's something out there!"

He was disoriented. Had he fallen asleep? Finn strained his eyes to see who was hovering over him. "Toni?" he asked in disbelief. "You're awake?" In the dim light, he could see that she had made a sling with her shirt, the tourniquet still tightly tied onto her forearm.

"I'm fine," she said through gritted teeth. "Don't worry about me. I think I can see something." Toni pointed a shaky finger in front of her.

In the hazy darkness, Finn saw a large shadow slowly moving towards them. He couldn't make out any of the features in the dim light of the stars and moon. It looked like a tall man.

"No way, I think it's a person," said Toni, slowly moving in front of Theodore who was fast asleep on the ground.

His heartbeat quickened.

The figure was well built and had a slight limp, weaving through the big boulders and cacti. Finn realized that they would be no match if this guy intended to hurt them; he was exhausted.

"Wake up, Theo, in case we have to make a run for it," she said out of the corner of her mouth. Toni must have come to the same realization but was not going down without a fight. She moved in front of them and picked up a large rock in her good hand, grunting with the effort of bending down. She looked ready to hurl it like a softball.

He was alarmed that Toni intended to protect them. She had just survived a mountain lion attack. Her wound might be infected, or the tourniquet might stop working and she could bleed out again. And it didn't help that she was breathing heavily from just a few movements.

The figure limped forward. Finn thought about all the fugitives and outlaws that might inhabit the desert. *We're going to be murdered,* he thought. "Theo, you have to wake up," he said, nudging him gently.

Theodore stirred and then closed his eyes again. He was red and sweaty, even in the freezing temperatures of the night.

Finn started to panic more. "Toni, he's not doing well. You're not doing well. Both of you need medical attention."

"I'll carry him then." She looked at him with a pained expression. She didn't know what else to do. Her fight or flight instinct compelled her to take the boys and escape.

Finn gave her an incredulous look. "Where are we going to go? We both know that you won't be able to carry him for long. You only have one good arm!" He struggled to keep his voice in a whisper. They had been through so much. They couldn't die here, not now. Finn knew that they had to make a decision—and quickly. The burly man was now 50 feet away. A crazy thought popped into his head. "Wait Toni, he might know where we can get help. Theodore is in trouble, and your arm might get worse."

She just looked at him like he was crazy. "He might be a serial killer!" She dropped her rock and started to pick up Theodore, clearly in pain. "We're leaving," she said firmly.

Finn opened his mouth to argue back.

My help comes in many forms. Follow him.

It was the same voice that had spoken to them on their first night in the bus.

Finn and Toni froze.

The voice had not come from the man who had now stopped 30 feet from the kids.

Finn gulped. They knew what to do. Together they propped up Theodore between them and stepped out of the circle of crosses.

CRUNCH

Finn looked down at his feet. He had stepped onto a shiny black scorpion. Finn jumped back, almost dropping Theodore. Toni grunted in pain as her arm jostled. She saw it too. They moved out of the way now realizing that there were dozens of black and brown scorpions littering the border of the circle.

All of them were dead.

Toni and Finn let out a collective gasp.

The circle of crosses had acted as a shield from the dangers of the desert.

Finn felt as if he was about to pass out but kept following the hunched figure. The figure, presumably a man, wore a long black robe, almost like a monk's garb. The man never wavered in guiding them, but Finn could hardly keep up. His feet hurt; he was severely dehydrated, even more so than when they ran out on day four. He could barely see in front of him because it was so dark. The moon was just a sliver in the sky, the stars just bright enough for Finn to see his shoes.

Shortly after they had begun their trek, Toni offered to take the full weight of Theodore. Relieved, Finn stumbled along behind them. He didn't know how Toni was able to carry Theodore with one arm. He admired her inner and outer strength. Maybe she had help.

Please God, please, please keep me and my friends safe. Keep Toni and Theodore safe. Please get us out of this desert. Amen. Finn's thoughts flickered from a pleading prayer to deductions about who this man was.

The figure didn't walk fast, but was just brisk enough so that they were never close enough to see who he was. He was tall and broad shouldered, and from what Finn could tell, strong. Thoughts on the identity of the man kept swirling in his head. *Who was he? It was God who led them to him, so he must be safe. Right?*

The inky blackness they walked in (for what felt like hours) receded into a pale dawn. On the horizon, he saw the sun begin its journey over the horizon. In this new light, Finn studied their guide. The man with a slight limp didn't wear a hat; his hair was white and curly. His hands and back of the neck were dark, and he carried a long walking stick. Just as Finn was scrutinizing the man, the figure glanced for a split second at Finn. Above the figure's white beard, dark eyes flashed bright and strong.

Finn tried to gulp but his throat was as dry as the sand beneath his feet. His tongue was even more swollen than when they had walked to the oasis. It was comforting to see the light, but if they had to keep walking during the daytime, he knew he wouldn't make it. It had been a full day since any of them had water or food, and they were burning calories fast. As they kept walking, Finn saw another small light in the distance.

Was he so dehydrated that he was seeing multiple versions of the sun? he thought to himself.

He looked ahead at his friends, but Theodore was in an even more dehydrated state. He slumped up against Toni as they kept walking. He could see that Toni was using all her energy to support Theodore. The man also seemed to notice the flickering light and began to lead the kids there. As they got closer and closer, Finn saw a figure laying down by the light, which he now realized was a flickering fire.

Finn realized who it was and stumbled over. "Andrew, Andrew, are you alright?" Finn asked in a raspy voice, his question barely audible, shaking his seemingly unconscious teacher.

"Check his pulse," croaked Toni, bending down beside Finn. They had put Theodore down in the sand near Andrew. He had slipped out of consciousness as soon as he laid down.

Finn felt for his wrist and felt a faint pulse.

It seemed that Andrew had built a fire, but there was no evidence that he had found more water other than the empty plastic water bottles Theodore had given him before he left the bus. The kids and Andrew were in the desert for five days.

How is Andrew alive right now? thought Finn. *We are barely alive right now, and we had multiple bottles of water.*

The figure slowly walked over to Andrew. The kids had forgotten that he was this close to them. Finn and Toni staggered out of the way and watched from the shadows. He placed a large dark hand on Andrew's head. Suddenly, Andrew groaned, and his eyes fluttered open. He looked around hazily, clearly not understanding what was happening.

The kids sighed with relief. Finn had a sense of new energy as he helped Toni prop their teacher up and continue following the man. Even though they found Andrew, Finn was exhausted and faltered as he tried to support Andrew. Toni noticed and took the full weight of their teacher with her good arm and nodded towards Theodore. Finn quickly grabbed his much lighter friend who was about to tip over. Finn gritted his teeth and put his head down as he kept trudging along. He still had hope that the tall figure would lead them to help.

The sun had now risen. With the added heat, it was almost too much for Toni to bear. She had always been able to excel in challenging circumstances—like when her team played a girl with the highest hit rate in the state and Toni struck her out, twice. But this, this heat and exhaustion and wound and stranger—she could collapse at any second. She prayed for strength.

Dear God, I know that I always think that I'm really strong, but right now I need the strength to get my friends to safety. Amen.

The desert landscape became an endless blur to Toni. There was no mystique in the sweeping cliffs and tall cacti. This was a quest for survival in an unforgiving land. Toni thought back to the Bible verse that her Tayta had above her door: "They wandered in the desert in the desolate way; They found no city to dwell in. Hungry and thirsty, their soul fainted in them. Then they cried out to the Lord in their trouble, and He delivered them out of their distresses."

How perfectly that Psalm fit their situation. Every time they were in trouble, every time something really bad happened, God saved them. Toni hoped that that would prove true in this case. *Probably,* she thought, *I mean, Saint Barbara comforted me after I passed out from my arm wound.*

Lost in thought Toni looked up. She gasped "Look ahead!" she rasped to her friends.

Finn wiped his soaked brown hair and squinted up. Then he saw it. A large, sturdy building with domes and crosses on the top. It was the monastery. In their excitement, the kids didn't realize that their mysterious guide disappeared as Finn used his last spurt of energy to thump on the heavy wooden door.

The door swung open and a monk with a scraggly beard gaped at the zombie-like kids propping up a semi-conscious man and boy.

Theodore slumped over.

"Thank you, Jesus," whispered Finn, as he fell to the ground in exhaustion.

They had made it.

Epilogue

"It's a miracle all four of them survived ... a real miracle ..." someone whispered.

Finn opened his eyes. He squinted against the bright lights that crept under his eyelids. Finn tried to lift his head but his body felt limp and heavy against the scratchy sheets.

"Easy buddy," said a soothing voice.

A woman with short brown hair stepped into his blurry vision.

"Mom?" croaked Finn.

He looked around through bleary eyes. To his right was his mom, and on the other side, his dad, brushing away a tear.

Where am I?

He thought back to the last thing he could remember.

The helicopter.

Theodore had been the first to collapse at the monastery door, his eyes sunken and his lips bleeding. From the ground he remembered the monk rushing inside to get help ... Toni slipping down onto the ground... their mysterious guide disappearing... his throat so dry it hurt ... his head pounding ... a red helicopter coming towards them.

And then everything was black.

Finn blinked and the memories faded. He looked

around. He was lying in a hospital bed with various tubes and needles in his arm and now his parents sat on either side of him, his mom stroking his arm.

Then it hit him. "Where's Toni and Theodore? Are they here? Are they okay? Is Andrew okay?" He looked around the small hospital room.

"Hey bud, don't worry!" his dad said. "Toni and Theodore and Andrew are all safe in the hospital. Andrew is being watched carefully for dehydration, but the doctors say he will be okay."

The horrifying image of seeing Andrew motionless on the desert floor flashed through his mind's eye. They had thought Andrew was dead.

"But you don't understand! Toni got attacked by a mountain lion—"

"Honey, she's doing fine now"; his mom cut in. "The doctor said that the surgery was successful and that she will have minimal long-term damage."

Minimal long-term damage. The thought of Toni never being able to play softball again made Finn want to curl up in a ball.

"And Theo ...? Is he okay?"

"He's also fine, thank God. His fever has broken and is getting an IV to rehydrate just like you," she said pointing to his arm.

"It's another miracle," his dad whispered.

"Dad, there were so many miracles, you don't even know about it," he said with eyes shining. "We wouldn't have survived if it weren't for literally all of Heaven. Saint

Hilaria and Saint Barbara and Saint Macrina and the angels and—oh the hermit! Mom! Call the monastery because I need to say thank you to the monk who saved us!"

His parents tilted their heads in a quizzical way.

"He was very tall, with white hair and darker skin."

"I know the monastery and the monks pretty well and I don't know a monk by that description, but I'll call them." His dad took out his phone and called.

"Hi … Yes, yes, thank God he's woken up … Thank you, Father … Yes, and the others are doing well … Yes, I know it's a miracle … *Abouna*, Finn is asking about the monk who helped them to the monastery? He says he's a hermit—tall, with white hair and dark skin … No? Oh. I see. Okay thank you so much *Abouna* … Yes, we'll stop by later, God willing … *Ma' al-salama.*" He put down his phone and looked up at Finn.

"He said there isn't a monk with that description. They don't even have hermits," said Finn's dad with a puzzled look.

"He helped me! I don't know who, but someone helped us," said Finn. Finn's parents looked at each other.

"We believe you, Finn," said his mom gently. His parents leaned onto Finn's bed and hugged him. "We're just so, so, so happy you made it," said Finn's dad.

Just then, the Saint Moses icon on Finn's bracelet glowed.

Glossary

Abouna	Arabic	Priest (literally "father")
Agpeya	Coptic	Prayer book split in different "hours" of the day (1st, 3rd, 6th, 9th, 11th)
Ful Mudammas	Arabic	Fava cooked beans
Gidu	Arabic	Grandfather
Intercessor / Intercession	English	Seeking a departed Christian, usually a saint, to pray for you
Liturgy	English	Church worship services
Ma' al-salama	Arabic	Goodbye (literally "with peace")
Synaxarion	Greek	Collection of saint biographies
Tasbeha	Arabic	Praises (hymns and prayers of worship and praise in the Coptic Orthodox Church)
Tayta	Arabic	Grandmother
Teen Shoki	Arabic	Prickly pear, cactus fruit
Thanksgiving Prayer	English	Common prayer of thanks in the Coptic Orthodox Church

Acknowledgments

"Every good and perfect gift is from above" (James 1:17). This book was truly a gift to write and to share. We wouldn't have been able to survive the desert of writing a book without all the wonderful people who made this book possible.

To the cloud of witnesses, our inspiration: Saints Hilaria, Barbara, Macrina, and Moses.

Our wonderful neighbor Dr. Elizabeth Dean encouraged us and read over our first drafts, braving the mosquitoes on our front porch to share her thoughts.

Thanks also to Sandra Mattar for her thoughtful insights and advice on publishing, Sherry Girguis for her support and perspective, and Yordanous Assefe for listening to all our crazy ideas.

Thank you to our priests at Saint Mark Coptic Orthodox Church and Fr. Peter Farrington for writing an accessible biography of Saint Hilaria.

Thank you to all of our English teachers who mentored and coached us over the years: Joy Korones, Catherine Ferrick, Lauren Arvis, and Kathleen Newman. Special thanks to our librarians for cultivating our love for books: Lynn Murphy, Alice Pleasants, and Kimberly Yeo.

We've enjoyed the kind of support and collaboration writers can only hope for in John Habib and all of the staff at the STM Abbey Press.

To our fabulous aunts, uncles, and cousins for pretending to be interested in our book. Just kidding.

Finally, we can't thank our mom and dad enough for

being our biggest cheerleaders, role models, and editors. This book wouldn't be possible without you. To our mom, Mimi, for answering all our questions, for dishing out the truth when we needed to hear it, and for pushing us to be our best selves. And to our dad, Robie, for instilling a sense of preparedness and for teaching us how to build our first fire. Thanks also to our little brother, Marky for providing inspiration and helping us with our research—you're writing the next book with us.

And of course, thanks to our very own Freddy Spaghetti, the most perfect 22-pound furry friend.

Lightning Source UK Ltd.
Milton Keynes UK
UKHW010628141222
413904UK00002B/398

9 781939 972446